# With a Fatal Whisper in My Ear, the Noose Dropped Over My Head...

But my first glimpse of the thrower was the very instant that the rope dropped over my head and gripped my arms. From that moment I was helpless and lay bewildered, while the very trees around me turned into madmen!

Not two or three men, but a full score leaped out around me, shrieking their triumph at one another and beating backs, thumping shoulders —almost too delighted with themselves to go ahead with the simple task of securing my hands behind me.

They tied me as though my flesh were fire and would burn through ordinary bonds. They swathed me in thirty or forty pounds of rope, and still some of the older men seemed a little anxious. But I had no thought of attempting to escape.

I looked about me on the bedlam with a sort of detached interest. It did not seem possible that I, Leon Porfilo, of Mendez, the son of the town butcher, the pupil of Father McGuire, should have attained such a bad eminence that so many brave and strong men could go half hysterical at the thought of it.

## Books by Max Brand

Published by POCKET BOOKS

# Max Brand

## SIX-GUN COUNTRY

PUBLISHED BY POCKET BOOKS NEW YORK

Originally published in *Western Story Magazine* in two installments: "The Outlaw Redeemer" and "His Fight for a Pardon."

POCKET BOOKS, a Simon & Schuster division of
GULF & WESTERN CORPORATION
1230 Avenue of the Americas, New York, N.Y. 10020

Published by arrangement with Dodd, Mead & Company, Inc.
Library of Congress Catalog Card Number: 79-24209

ISBN: 0-671-41516-6

First Pocket Books printing May, 1981

10  9  8  7  6  5  4  3  2  1

POCKET and colophon are trademarks of Simon & Schuster.

Printed in the U.S.A.

# SIX-GUN COUNTRY

# ··· 1 ···

In all the time I had been hunted by the law, I had had no apprehension quite like that which I experienced when I learned that Andrew Chase had come into the hills to fight it out with me.

I could not get it out of my head that Andrew was invincible, for he had been more than a hero in my eyes ever since that day when he had knocked me flat into the dust after I had fought a fair fight with his brother Harry, and for the second time gained a victory that Harry would have given a great deal to have won.

Now you will remember that I was properly convinced that Andrew Chase was at the bottom of all this mess that I was in. After I had stood up against his brother, Harry, in a gun fight, and come out of the battle unscathed, Andrew had taken the situation into his own hands.

Then there had followed the hiring of Turk Niginski, a gunman, whose services had been bought to put me out of the way, for, reasoned Andrew, it was better that I should die than that his brother should face my weapons again and lose his life.

But Niginski had failed in his undertaking, and you will remember how I had whirled in the saddle and shot him dead, and then ridden straight to the sheriff with my true story of self-defense.

There had followed the trial, and my conviction and sentence to twenty-five years' imprisonment. Not even Father McGuire, with whom I had lived since the age of fourteen, could do anything for me. It remained for Tex Cummins, at that time a perfect stranger to me, to plan my escape and furnish me with a mount with which to make my getaway into the hills.

It was upon that first ride away from pursuit as a fugitive of the law that I met Margaret O'Rourke, "Mike" as I called her, and had fallen promptly in love with her.

So when I had heard that Andrew Chase had come into the hills to get me, and had learned further that he had had the audacity to make friends with Mike, I had promptly warned her to beware of Andrew Chase, that he was not to be trusted. Whereupon we had had a falling out, and I had gotten myself deeper into the entanglements with the law by my headlong rush into more mischief.

Then had come the message that Mike wished to see me, and my heart had swelled within me, only to have my hopes as quickly dashed upon the rocks by her announcement that she loved Andrew Chase and that she had sent for me to exact a promise from me not to fight him for fear that he might lose his life. From that moment I had promptly become a madman, had rushed out into the night, only to meet Andrew and to thrash him to within an inch of his life.

Then I had brought him, torn and bleeding, to Mike.

After I heard that Andrew Chase had gained enough strength to leave the bed into which I had put him, and when I heard that, in shame because he could not face the men of the mountains, and because he dared not return to his home in Mendez, he had ridden east; after I heard all this news, I decided to go to see Margaret O'Rourke and ask her, frankly, what chance I had with her.

It was not, really, that I wished to gloat over her because the man she had chosen to love had turned out a rascal—or a rascal to a certain degree, at least. But I knew that Margaret O'Rourke was too brave and too kind and too honest to leave me in doubt as to whether or not I had any hope of winning her in the end. If I had not the shadow of a chance, I frankly wished to tell her that I would never see her face again.

I had had to learn to make decisions and abide by them before. It was now three years since I had lived outside of the law with a price on my head, and the only reason that I had been able to avoid the long arm of the law, I very well knew, was that I had made certain resolutions and stuck grimly to them.

Above all, for instance, I had decided early in my career that I would never associate myself with a partner. For one may be sure of oneself, but never of one's companion, and I had heard of and seen too many keen, alert, intelligent men who could not defy the law because they could not live without companionship. Their companion always proved the weaker link by which their strength was broken.

It was a bitter thing to live like a lone wolf in the mountains through all manner of weather, ever on the alert, and never leaving my secure retreats unless there was an absolute need to go down among other men for the sake of food or of money.

I had clung to that schedule for three years, and the result was that the headhunters had gone without my scalp.

When a man has denied himself human companionship and human liberty, it is possible for him to forswear even the joy of seeing the woman he loves.

With that in mind, I saddled Roanoke and went down to see Margaret O'Rourke.

I rode through the day until I was in the forest at the edge of the big valley. Then, in the dusk, I sent Roanoke down the steep descent to the floor of the valley itself—a dizzy pitch which no horse could have negotiated, but the mule, as a mountain flyer, was to the manner born. He skidded or bounced down the ragged slopes and then bore me across the valley at his swinging trot.

I came up the ravine where O'Rourke lived, in the black heart of the night. It was no longer necessary for me to whistle my signal from beneath the trees opposite the house. All I had to do was to make sure that no one was in the house except the family. They knew me now, and I felt that I knew them well enough to trust them—once in a long while!

For, other than upon exceptional occasions, there were only three people in the world whom I would really trust, and they were Sheriff Dick Lawton, Father McGuire, and Margaret O'Rourke herself. An odd assemblage for an outlaw to know, you may say!

So I left Roanoke under the trees, picking at the grass in the darkness, and I went across to the house to scout around. I looked in the dining room first, to see if Pat O'Rourke had any callers. There were none. He sat in one chair with his boots scarring the cane bottom of another chair, and the newspaper spread in front of him.

But I was fairly certain that Margaret herself was entertaining company, for I could hear her singing and playing the piano in the parlor. Certainly she would not be so gay except for the sake of another person—not when it was a scant fortnight since the man she loved had left the house.

I slipped up onto the porch and peeked in under the bottom of the shade. I could hardly believe my eyes when I saw that she was alone in the room, with her head tilted back, singing like a bird!

So I went to the front door and tapped softly. She opened it a moment later, and when she saw me, she cried out happily and drew me into the room.

"I thought that you were never coming again, Leon," said she.

"I wasn't sure that you'd ever want to see me again," I explained.

"You might take off your hat," said she.

I snatched it off. One can't be three years in the high rocks and remember all the amenities of polite society.

"Confound it, Mike," said I, getting a little red, "you might give me time to get my bearings."

She looked me up and down, surveying my ragged clothes and the two guns strapped at my hips and the Indian brown of my face and hands; and she smiled her crooked smile, which sank a dimple exactly in the center of one cheek.

"There you are," said Mike. "You haven't been here ten seconds—and you begin to fight so soon!"

"That's not fair," said I. "I came—"

"Well, sit down," said she. "Shall I let the family know that you're here?"

"Darn the family," said I. "I want you. I've gone on

short rations for a long time so far as seeing you is concerned."

She sat down on the piano bench, still studying me.

"You're bigger than ever, Lee," said she.

"What I've come to say—" I began again.

"And that frown," said she, "is getting to be a habit."

"All right," said I, settling back with a sigh, "when you're through looking me over, I'll try to talk."

"There is to be a pardon granted to you, isn't there?" she asked. "I understand that Sheriff Lawton is doing a great deal to square you with the law."

"I don't know. I don't dare to think about it."

"Everyone else is thinking, though," said she. "We hear that Sheriff Lawton has made a trip to see the governor and talk to him about you."

"Sheriff Lawton is an honest man!" said I.

"Then there's word that Father McGuire has gone from Mendez to back up Lawton with the governor."

"God bless Father McGuire," said I. "I'd rather have his good word than be president of the United States!"

"But all the trouble is going to end, Lee. Oh, how glad I am! It's making an old man of you!"

"What I want to know," said I, "is just exactly how glad you are."

"Nobody in the world could be happier about it," said she.

"Wait a minute," said I, feeling that old, wild hope surge up in me. "Think that over before you say it."

She answered gently: "Unless you've found a girl to marry you, Leon Porfilo."

"I've found the only girl that I can ever marry," said I, very solemn. "That's what I came down here to talk about."

She shook her head.

"Oh," I explained, "I don't mean that I want any promises. I want a chance to hope. That's all."

She said nothing, but looked at me sadly and thoughtfully.

"When I heard you singing so happily," said I, "I thought you might have decided to forget him."

"I can never forget Andrew," said Mike.

"Then that's the end for me," said I, and stood up.

"Lee," said she, "are you really going to run off again with only two words spoken between us?"

"Well, why should I talk?" said I.

"Are we at least friends?" she asked me.

"No," said I. "Either I have a hope to have you someday as my wife, or else I'll never see your face again. I'll go no half measures and torment myself for years. Either I'll have a hope, or I have no hope at all!"

"Am I to tell you just what you mean to me?" she asked.

"Yes, if you will."

"Of course I will. I've always loved you, Lee, since the first day I put eyes on you."

"That's a fair start," said I without enthusiasm. "That's a pretty good opening. You always loved me, so you decided to marry another man?"

"There are all sorts of love," said she. "Andrew Chase took me off my feet. When you came down to kill him—or he you—I suppose that I hated you, for a while. But now he's gone."

"For good?"

"I suppose so."

"Mike, do you really expect that you'll never see him again? Do you care?"

She studied the floor for a moment and spoke with her head still bent down.

"A year ago I would have said that I would despise

forever any man who did to Leon Porfilo such a dastardly thing as Andrew did to you in hiring Turk Niginski. Well, since Andrew left, I have thought it over and tried to look at it and at myself frankly. I am ashamed to confess that I do not despise him, Lee. Or, if I despise him, I'm almost fonder of him than ever. Can you understand that?"

"I cannot," said I bluntly.

"I don't suppose you can. You're a man all fire and iron. You want everything or nothing. But women aren't that way, you know. They hardly know what they want in a man, I suppose. But I know this—that I don't want to give you up, Leon! I think of Andrew once a day, and the thought of him makes my heart jump. I think of you every minute, and it always makes me happy—quietly happy. But I know that isn't enough for you."

"It isn't," said I bitterly. "I think of my mule, Roanoke, and it makes me quietly happy. But I want something more than that. I've got to have something more than that! Can you give it to me, Mike?"

"I've told you everything," said she.

"It's not enough," said I, dragging the words up from the roots of my heart. "I'm going to shut out the thought of you, Mike. I've got to do it."

She turned half away from me.

"Mike," said I, holding out my hand, "good-by."

She murmured swiftly: "Will you go quickly—before I start crying like a silly little fool?"

I jammed my hat on my head and strode out of that house, never to see it again, I thought.

## ... 2 ...

One cannot be forever cautious. Besides, when I left
Mike O'Rourke, I was so full of my vow never to see
her again, but to shut her firmly from my life, that I
did not much care what became of me. I turned Roanoke up the valley and rode straight on at the lights of
the town!

It was not such complete madness as you might
imagine, because since it was so generally believed that
the governor was about to grant me a pardon—what
with the good offices of Sheriff Lawton and half a
dozen other prominent people on the range—the boys
were not so keen to hunt me as they had been before.

They could not be sure, you see, that when they
risked their lives to get me, they were not hunting
down a man whom a proclamation had cleared of all
crime.

I was fairly sure, therefore, that I underwent no real
risk in venturing into Sanburn. There was no reason

why the people in that town should have a peculiar grudge against me! In fact, I could not recall that I had ever harmed any one of the citizens.

So I let Roanoke drift boldly into the little village, only pulling him aside from the main street and putting him through a side alley. We turned a corner into a huddle of noise and cursing. The Sanburn stagecoach was rolling down the street surrounded by a score of excited horsemen; and from the interior of the coach, now and then, heavy groans reached my ear.

I had only time to hear and see this much when someone shouted:

"He's come back to see what trouble he's raised! Let's get him, boys!"

He who raised the shout fairly led the way by sending a .45-caliber slug through the brim of my sombrero. I could not imagine what the confusion was about, but I did not stay to ask questions. Roanoke turned like a cat, and I drove him through a narrow gap between two houses. There he wove back and forth among boxes and cans, leaped a high back fence, and took me into the open running beyond.

I heard the pursuit crashing and raving among the obstacles in that narrow alley. But the greater part of those hot riders had not tried the narrow pass at all, but spilled out on either side and came combing out after me by more roundabout ways. I gave Roanoke his head, and he streaked away.

He had as much foot as a good cow pony—but no more. When it came to a narrow brush like this one, I was much worried. I could only hope that there were no blood horses in that crew behind me to sprint up to us. There *were* some fast nags, however. Three men began to draw up with me, but they were in no hurry to close. I sent one bullet blindly into the sky above their heads, and they drew back.

By the time they had rallied enough heart to decide to rush down on me again, their fast horses were beginning to be half winded, whereas Roanoke was running as easily as ever. That extraordinary mule could not raise himself above a certain top speed, but he could maintain his top pitch for an uncanny length of time.

So it was now. He held them even for another mile, until we hit the foothills, and after that they were done.

What I wondered at, however, was the venom which had brought these fellows out humming after me. Still I could hear their angry shouts as I galloped Roanoke over the first hill crest. Then we sloped down into the dimness beyond, and I knew that I was safe.

However, I was not content with being safe. I wanted to know what lay at the bottom of this explosion. But I had to keep my impatience with me for a full three days before I learned what I wanted to know. Then I got it from the pages of the Sanburn newspaper.

They had spilled it across their whole front page. News was shy that week, I suppose, for they gave most of the issue to me and my unlucky career.

But they opened up with the following flare:

NEW OUTRAGE BY LEON PORFILO
OUTLAW TURNS STAGE ROBBER
SANBURN STAGE STOPPED
THREE MEN BRUTALLY SHOT DOWN!

That was the opening. What followed was enough to bear out the headlines. The Sanburn stage had been stopped by a tall man riding a mouse-colored mule like Roanoke. He wore a mask and announced that he was Leon Porfilo and that he was tired of waiting for the governor's pardon, and had decided to fill his empty pockets.

Empty pockets, when I had more than four thousand in my wallet at that moment!

It appeared that my ghost had stopped the stage and ordered the passengers out. But these passengers had too much spot cash on them and too many guns and the courage to use them to submit calmly to such a summons. Someone paved the way by dropping to the dust of the road on his belly and blazing away at the sham Porfilo. There were two others who followed suit.

I gathered that if this imitator of mine were a grand liar, he was at least a great fighter, also. For he had dropped those three worthies one after another. Two were badly wounded. One was dangerously shot and might die.

That was the first item of this story. The rest was what might be expected. The governor not only refused to consider my pardon any longer, but he had issued a ringing declaration that he would see that the laws of this State were obeyed and that he would have Leon Porfilo, outlaw, robber, murderer, out of the mountains if he had to call up every man of the militia.

It made me sweat a little, but I could not help grinning when I thought of raw militia boys struggling through the mountains and broiling on the bleak mountains while I was tucked away securely watching the fun. I was not afraid that they would take me.

They had almost as much chance of taking an eagle with their bare hands, for I had been hunted over every inch of that range during the last three years, and I knew the whole country. I could take it to pieces in my mind and put it together again, you might say. Every bird's nest in the region above timberline was pretty familiarly known to me.

Besides, and above all, I had that king of mules, Roanoke, to float me over cliffs like a bird on wings.

So I was not particularly disturbed by the governor's threats. The last governor before him had made threats just as big and announcements just as cocksure. But there were other elements which were not so pleasant. In the first place, I had been robbed of my expected pardon. In the second place, there had been an instant response to this most recent Porfilo "outrage," and the price on my head was a full fifteen thousand dollars!

Now, out West, where a man will work like a dog all of every day and a share of every night for a beggarly fifty a month, fifteen thousand dollars in a lump is like the dream of a gold mine. I knew that I should have to pass through a period like that which had tormented me long before when a price was first put on my head and the mountaineers had not yet learned to have some fear of me.

But what moved me most of all was rage at the scoundrel who had dared to use my name in order to help him in the robbery of the coach.

For my part, I had never attempted a deed so terribly bold as such a holdup. In the second place, I had never dreamed of such a thing as shooting down three inoffensive men who were merely striving to protect their own rights. I thought of the matter in another light, also. When Mike O'Rourke heard the story, she would believe that I had left her determined upon mischief, and she would believe that this bloodthirsty thing was all my work!

What I determined upon was to corner the rascal at once and wring a signed confession from him—or at the least have the satisfaction of filling him full of lead. No, to shoot him down would be no satisfaction at all. It would merely remove my last chance of proving my innocence.

I sat down to figure out the trail of the robber. That may seem odd to you, but as I have said before, I knew those mountains more intimately than any student can know the pages of a book. I closed my eyes and summoned the picture. Then I opened them again and drew out the scene in the sand. I had no sooner done that than one fact jumped into my mind at once—this robber was a fellow who did not know the country at all!

He had selected for the holdup site a spot where the trail dipped, beside the Sanburn River, into a long and narrow valley on either side of which gorges cut away from the river. But the ends of all those gorges were impractical for any animal less adroit of foot than Roanoke, say.

All that an organized pursuit would have had to do would have been to sweep up and down that valley at once and the robber was fairly bottled. The only reason that they had not adopted that measure was that they were fairly certain that if the robber were indeed Leon Porfilo, he would never commit a robbery in such a difficult spot.

If this man had really been aware of the nature of the country, he would have selected a spot on the road where it wound through the badlands of the upper plateau. I could have sworn that this stranger selected the eventual site of the holdup simply because he was sure those side ravines were routes by which he could easily ascend to the upper mountains.

The upper mountains, then, were his goal.

It was a bewildering region, as I knew by many a bitter experience, until I mapped it for myself. Even old mountaineers did not like to cross that section of

the hills without a good guide, because the face of the
land was knifed across by an intricate crisscrossing of
ravines. Men had been known to wander about for
half a month before they drew clear of those entan-
gled chasms and blind alleys among the mountains;
and in the cold of the winter more than one poor fellow had lost his life in that region.

As for the fellow who had dared to take up my role
and play stage robber under my name, I could not
help wondering just how he had solved the problem
of the ravines! What I felt was that he would probably
work grimly and patiently north, guided by the crest
of one of the taller mountains. If he was cool enough
to shoot three men in one fight, he was cool enough to
stick by one landmark.

So, with all these things in mind, I cut across the
high country and made straight for Danny Chisholm's
camp.

## ••• 3 •••

Chisholm's was a strictly summer camp. Half the year it was buried in frightful snowdrifts that sagged through the gulch to the north of his place. Six months of the year there were anywhere from five to fifty feet of snow rolled on top of the Chisholm shack. When the first white weather began, Danny Chisholm cached everything in wrappings of oilcloth, put some heavy props under the roofs of his sheds, prayed that they would hold the weight of the snows until the next thaw, and then trekked down for the lowlands.

So the camp slept under sheeted ice and snow during six months of the year, but the remaining six months it was a sort of open-air hotel. It was a queer sort of crossroads that he had chosen for his camp. There were no main trails that passed up and down or across the ridges at this point, but trappers, hunters, botanists, and the bolder spirits among the tourists who loved the high places crossed and recrossed the site of the Chisholm camp.

Besides, there were certain other enforced travelers —as one might call them—who dropped in at Chrisholm's. These were men who did not wish to give names, who did not wish to ask questions or answer them. Chisholm was famous for the absence of embarrassing conversation at his camp fire. Altogether, what with one class of traveler and another, Danny made a pretty penny during the warmer seasons of the year.

I came over the south shoulder of Mount Christmas and in the hollow beneath me was the glimmer of the Chisholm fire, made into a single thin ray of red light. I followed it like a star, until I was close to his clearing. Then, at a little distance, I put up Roanoke in an open space where he would find plenty of forage, and went on foot toward the fire. I had slung a pack across my back, so that I could fill the part of a foot traveler.

What I first saw from the shadows of the trees at the edge of the clearing was the active figure of Danny Chisholm. That little man never rested. He was forever cooking or cleaning up, or whirling about like a squirrel on a branch to ask one of his guests if they were comfortable.

Usually, as tonight, his guests slept in the open. In case of need, they could be lodged in very foul weather under one of his damp, tumbledown sheds. Now their blankets were spread in the outer rim of the firelight. In the air was the last tang of coffee which had been made for the latest comer. There was a rumbling of deep, contented voices; and when a puff of wind came, it never failed to raise a sharp tongue of flame that cast a bright wink of light over the clearing and made the nearest pine trees glisten.

I stood there for a moment, enjoying the scene, and the great upper peaks which walked up among the stars in the distance. I felt like a tiny Tom Thumb in the hollow hand of a giant.

Then I noticed the other guests. There were only three of them—one young, and two big-shouldered mountaineers with beards of uncertain date shrouding their faces. As for me, I remained where I was, in the shadow.

For there was never any trace of me, even in a place like Danny Chisholm's, where ordinary strifes were forgotten. This was a court of last resource to which all men resorted when they were hard pressed by wind and weather. The lion and the lamb lay down together in actual fact, and if there were occasional quarrels here, they were the quarrels which originated in the camp itself, and which were not imported from the outside.

But even this atmosphere of truce I could not trust. No unwritten law was strong enough to protect a man with fifteen thousand dollars on his head! For a moment, a great bitterness went through me.

In the old days I was very often set up with a feeling of grandeur because of my very loneliness; but as time went on, that loneliness ate into my spirit, and often a convulsion of something like homesickness made me as weak as a child.

Danny Chisholm came to me at once. When he saw that I preferred the shadows, he did not urge me to come closer to the camp fire. I asked him if he had a cup of coffee left, and he went hastily for it and brought me back a great slab of pone, split open and layered with molasses inside. It tasted better than any cake I have ever touched, and the coffee of another man's making was nectar to me.

I sat with my back to the tree behind me and drank and ate. Danny Chisholm stood near by and talked—about a tenderfoot who had come up to his camp bent on shooting a mountain sheep, about Dad Riley coming in with a load of moonshine, about a new rifle which he had bought, and about the Sanburn holdup.

He chatted on in an easy monotone, never waiting for a reply, only pausing to puff in leisurely fashion at his pipe. But he knew that I was hungry to hear him, as any man who lives like a hermit against his will begins to hunger for the sound of a human voice. To me, that foolish babble was sweeter than wine and honey. It relaxed me, body and soul, and it made me almost sleepy with content. It filled me with an immense good will to fellow men.

Then voices began to be heard beside the camp fire, and Danny hastened back to it.

He stood, ridiculously small in the flare of the fire, gesticulating with both hands. Those three big fellows, each was almost as tall, sitting, as was Danny on his feet.

"I got only one thing to say," said Danny. "If you've come here for a fight, go off somewhere and fight where the loser'll roll into the river where he drops. I disremember what year it was when the Slocum boys come up here and got into a scrap with a couple of old sourdoughs. Two of 'em was killed; two more was laid up. I had to bury them that died—right here in these rocks.

"It was like breaking ground in quartzite. Besides, I had to nurse them two that was down. What did I get out of it? Nothing at all! They was all broke. The pickings in their pockets wasn't enough to feed a layin' hen through the summer season! So I say: If you want to fight, go out where the mountains can see you. I'm too old to be interested in that sort of a show!"

Danny was really what one might call hard-boiled. He never pretended that he had any ultimate interest in his guests beyond getting their money. Everyone liked his frankness.

One of the bearded fellows took up the talk, and at the first word I pricked up my ears.

"Porfilo," said he. "That was what we was talking about. This kid—"

"Porfilo," put in Danny Chisholm, "is a poor thing to talk about day or night, in the valley or up here in the mountains. Because you never know what side folks is gunna take about him."

"Look here," said the bearded man, "there *used* to be two sides. The best side used to be the one that figgered he'd done nothin' that wasn't overbalanced by the good he's done. I was one of them that stood on that side. But along comes this here stage holdup —and that's different!"

"Why different?" put in the youth.

Now he sat up and squared his shoulders and turned his head a little. I saw that he was a whale of a man, boy, rather. For the firelight, streaking down his profile, showed me a fine-looking youngster of not more than eighteen, the sort of eighteen-year-old who has stepped into nearly his full strength.

I had been that sort of a boy. Three long years ago I had been as he was now. One sees such fellows fighting in the prize ring, from time to time, powerful as men but supple as children, recuperating swiftly after hard blows, full of zest and battle.

I, from the altitude of twenty-one, looked with an almost sad wisdom upon this boy. Not three years, but three decades stretched between us.

"There you are," said Chisholm. "You see that you got an argument pronto. Ain't I right about it?"

"This here—kid," said the first speaker, making a little pause of contempt before he named the boy, "is arguin' like a plumb fool. He don't see no difference between what Porfilo has done before and what he's done this time."

"He busted into a house and slammed three men, all on one night," said the boy.

"That was with his fists."

"Well, is guns any worse?"

"Worse by just a mite. Just the mite of difference between livin' and dyin'. "

"Who did he kill when he stuck up the stage?"

"By luck he didn't kill none—but he shot three times to kill. One slug just missed the heart of one of the boys. Another plowed through the cheek and tore off the ear of another chap. Them bullets was aimed to kill, which is something that he never done before, except when his back was agin' the wall!"

The boy jerked back his head. "His back was agin' the wall when he held up the stage!"

"How come?"

"They stuck up their hands, and when he lowered his gun, one of 'em made a phony move and started shootin'. They deserved to die, all the three of 'em, for tryin' a double cross!"

"Is that your way of lookin' at it, kid?" said the burly fellow who carried on the brunt of the talk for the other side. "Well, then I got to say that you're gunna make a fine sort of a citizen, one of these days."

"I dunno that I like the way that you say that!" said the boy.

But the other two did not understand. What they heard in his voice was a tremor which was very pronounced and which was exactly like the tremor of fear. But I knew better.

Indeed, there was fear in that youngster, but it was the sort of fear which drives men into the deeds of most frantic heroism. It was the fear which a man feels when he is in doubt about himself. Fear that he will not do all that can be expected of a man.

The instant I heard that tremor in the throat of the boy, I gathered my feet under me and got ready to jump behind a tree out of the path of possible bullets, for I knew that trouble was coming.

Then the bearded rascal brought all to a climax by snorting:

"*You* don't like it? Then what'll you do about it?"

# ··· 4 ···

There was no delay. The boy leaped to his feet.

He was a glorious thing to look at. Opposite him two burly men rolled up and stood braced for action. They were not so tall, not so nimble—but they were as tough and as jagged as the rocks among which they had been moiling all their lives. Under those beards were jaws of iron, broad cheekbones. Under their clothes were muscles like slabs of India rubber. They had great arched breasts, and the strength of their arms made them carry their hands far from their sides.

"I'll do this, to start with," said the youngster, as he dashed his fist into a beard and reached the jawbone beneath and sent one foeman staggering.

I have no doubt, from his fine bearing, that he meant nothing but the best of fair play, for his part. But there was no sense for such matters in the other two. One of them lunged in instantly from the other side and, grappling the boy around the body, carried him to the earth by the shock of his rushing weight.

Neither did these cold-hearted devils mean to let him get to his feet. The first man, shaking the daze out of his head, came striding back.

"Hold him down, Pete!" he snarled. "We'll give him something to think about!"

"You coyotes!" groaned the boy. "Lemme get up, and I'll fight the two of you fair and square!"

He meant it, too. That was enough for me. I had promised myself that no matter how the fight went, I should not show my face. But this was too much for me. I came to my feet and joined that fracas with a rush. I sent a battle cry before me, and the first man wheeled to meet my charge. He put up his hands in good enough posture, but then the firelight struck bright into my eyes, and I heard him shout: "Porfilo!"

It seemed to drain all the strength out of him. It was not a man but a statue of putty that I put my fist into. He went down in a crumbling heap.

His shout released the boy, too. For when the second mountaineer heard my name, he leaped to his feet and sprinted for the woods.

"Porfilo!" said the boy, and sat up with a gasp. "It *is* Porfilo!" he breathed.

"Get back into the shadow," I commanded him, and tugged him to his feet with a jerk. "Get back among the trees, before the pair of them try to pick us off from cover!"

We hurried back into the shadows, but there seemed little doubt about what the two men of the mountains would do. They were rushing off as fast as their legs would carry them; as though they had called on the devil—and raised him quite beyond their expectations! Far away, we heard the crashing of the brush as they sprinted on.

"Porfilo," said the boy, "darned if I ain't sorry that I got you mixed into this mess."

He was not as sorry as I was, however. For, every time I had to step into such a fight, it meant that I made not two enemies, but two hundred. Every new story of violence that was repeated about me went up and down through the mountains and turned the minds of many honest, peace-loving men against me.

"What's your name?" I asked him, very, very heavy with all of these reflections.

"Orton," said he.

"Your first name?" said I.

"Dick."

"Dick, you're a young fool!"

I heard him gasp an indrawn breath. "Porfilo," said he at last, in a voice as thin as the voice of a frightened child, "that's a good deal to take from any man—even from you."

"Is it?" said I, still very angry.

"Too much," said he. "I can't swaller it!"

Then I saw what was in his mind. I had been too sick at heart to understand, before.

"What do you want me to do?" said I.

"Apologize!" said Dick Orton. "Or I'll—"

Yes, there he was ready for it already! His head was back and his body was trembling as much as his voice.

"Oh, the devil!" said I. "I'll apologize, of course. I'm sorry I hurt your feelings, Dick!"

This was a great deal too much for him. There was not much light from the fire in the shadows where we stood, but there was enough for me to see the glassy rolling of Dick Orton's eyes.

"You're joking, Porfilo!" said he.

"Not a bit," said I.

"You're tryin' to make a fool out of me," said he.

"Not at all," said I.

"Porfilo wouldn't apologize to nobody but the devil himself!" said this silly boy.

"Who has been filling your head full of nonsense about me?" I asked him.

He stepped a little closer to me to study me. "You *are* Porfilo," said he, as though there could ever be any doubt as to the identity of my ugly, prizefighter's face.

"I'm Porfilo," I repeated. "I've apologized for hurting your feelings. Is that apology enough?"

"Ah," said Dick Orton, "I didn't mean to ask you to—I mean that I was in the wrong—"

"Of course you were!" said I.

"Then why did you ask my pardon?"

"Because I didn't want to fight."

There was no way of handling that young fool without being in danger. He was worse than a bundle of nettles.

"I'm too small for you, maybe?" says he, lifting his head to his full height.

He was about half an inch taller than I.

"Or maybe," said he, "you figger out that I'm just a kid and that I ought to be home helpin' Ma with the supper dishes. Is that it?"

I had picked up my pack and now I flung it over my shoulders and turned my back on him and strode away as fast as I could. Because he had gone far enough to anger me in spite of all my efforts at self-control. In those days I felt that I was quite a world-weary man, but I can look back at myself and see that I was a good deal of a child. However, that young idiot would have irritated a saint.

I left him behind and made for my Roanoke with a very hearty wish that Chisholm's place and everybody in it were in the hands of the devil. Just as I reached the clearing where I had left Roanoke, there was a crashing behind me, and that young giant blundered out into the open starlight. More than starlight. The moon was somewhere, sifting thin shadows of the trees across the ground and showing me the face of Dick Orton.

"I'm not good enough to get an answer?" said he.

He stood before me with his feet braced and his body bent a little; he was full of that same devil of fear that had made him fight the two at Chisholm's camp a little before.

"Orton," said I at last with a groan, "do you want me to get down on my knees and beg you not to shoot me?"

Because he had come to that point. One hand, shaking with passion, was fluttering at his right hip, touching the butt of his gun and hovering away from it again in little jerky movements.

He was staggered again by what I said. He could not understand. So I added: "Do you want me to breathe flame and eat iron? I'm a peaceable man, Orton, until fellows like you crowd my back to the wall. All I'm saying is: For Lord's sake give me a chance to be friendly!"

Dick Orton gasped. Then his eyes rolled from side to side, as though, under the skin of a dragon, he had found a child.

Then, "There's Roanoke!" he cried softly. "By jiminy, I've been wanting to see Roanoke—and there he is! You *are* Porfilo, no matter how you talk!"

Yes, in spite of what he had seen and heard, he had still been in doubt as to my identity. I was a thousand times too humble to fit in with his preconceived idea of me.

Then he blurted out: "Porfilo, I guess that I've been acting like a fool!"

"I'm afraid to say yes," said I. "Or you'd have a gun out at me!"

"I was scared to death," said he, "but I thought that you were talkin' down to me."

"I'd as soon talk down to a snowslide that was aimed straight at my head," I said.

I mopped away the perspiration from my face. In fact, I had had a rather nerve-racking passage with this young fire-eater.

"Well," he said, "I want to know if you'll forgive me."

"Sure," said I. "Thank heaven that there's no harm done—to either of us!"

"Will you do one thing more for me?"

"Yes," said I, not pausing to think.

"Then let me ride along with you for a day."

"What the devil are you asking for?" I growled at him. "Trouble?"

"You've given me your promise," said he.

"Darn a promise!" said I. "If you ride with an out-lawed man—"

"I'd rather ride with you than with a king, Porfilo!" says he.

I saw how the wind lay.

"I have your promise!" he cried, very exultant. "You can't go back on that!"

"Well," said I at last, "go get your horse!"

He was gone in a flash, and I, cursing steadily, put the saddle on Roanoke, because it was not wise to stay near Chisholm's after that evening's scene.

I turned from my work, a moment later, and saw Dick Orton ride into the clearing, and he was on the back of another mule!

I did not have to possess the wits of a detective to put two and two together now. It was perfectly plain me that Richard Orton, like a dizzy-headed young had read of the adventures of Leon Porfilo and out to parallel them.

But the very first thing he had done was more fool-hardy than all of my adventures put together and rolled into one. For it was he who had ridden a mule to hold up the stage, and who had posed as the possessor of my name.

Here was I, who had started out with a hot hatred to find the pretender and destroy him—here was I helpless and buried in gloom. I could not help liking this young idiot. I could not help it. Neither could I say a word to him about the frightful wrong that he had done me for fear he would do some equally insane and romantic act.

If I pointed out to him that this stage robbery had robbed me, at the same time, of my chance to get a State pardon, beyond a doubt he would scurry down to give himself up, confess his crime, and be promptly thrown into prison for the better half of his remaining life!

What was I to do?

I did not know. I wanted to be just to this madman; but I was also hungry to have justice for myself. I decided to go to get advice as quickly as I could.

My companion in the meantime jogged his mule at my side as contented as he could be. We came to a cliff as bare as the palm of my hand.

"Are you going down it?" said Dick, as serious as you please.

I turned and gaped at him. Even a mountain goat would have been dizzy for a month at the mere thought of that precipice.

"Where are my wings, Dick?" said I.

"Why," he muttered in a rather complaining way, "I thought that nothing could stop Roanoke!"

"Roanoke is like me," said I. "Overpraised! A darn sight overpraised!"

But Dick merely shook his head. His idea of me

and of that tough-mouthed mule I rode was too deeply fixed in him to be changed by mere words!

I turned up along the edge of that cliff and hit for the higher ground because I had my plan for the night's campaign firmly in mind. On the way, I drew him into talk. Although he seemed to be bubbling over with a desire to hear me chatter about myself, he was young enough to be willing to speak of himself.

"What started you for the high spots, Dick?" said I.

"Hearing about the good things you've been having for the last five or six years," said he.

"Three years!" I corrected him. "Three years, Dick."

"Is that all? Seems to me I can hardly remember when they were not talking about Leon Porfilo."

"As for the good times——" But I could not continue in that strain. How could I tell him about the bitter loneliness of the mountains? How could I tell him of that weak yearning which went like water through my blood a thousand times—the yearning to have other men around me? No, I decided that words could never turn the trick. The more I talked, the more glamour he would feel in what I had to say.

So I changed the theme.

"But there was something more than what you had heard of me that made you go wild," I declared. "What else lies behind it?"

"The old man," said he.

"Explain that."

"The old man," said Dick, "started out selling newspapers in New York. He wound up on a ranch, with plenty of hosses and plenty of coin, but the things that he figgers count the most are the things that he got locked up inside his head while he was stamping his feet to keep the chilblains out of his toes, and shoving papers under the noses of gents on Broadway.

"Back yonder, the big guns are the doctors and the lawyers, and suchlike things. What he has mapped out for me is a lawyer's desk. Me!"

He threw out his arms and laughed. The gesture startled his mule, and the foolish thing began to buck on the edge of the cliff. I was so thoroughly frightened that I could hardly look. But Dick Orton merely laughed and threw spurs and quirt into his nag to make it buck still harder—all of this with perdition six inches away.

Then the mule had enough, and jogged on its way again.

Certainly I had seen enough of this youngster to demonstrate to me that the man who tried to control him was rather thick in the head. I would as soon try to plan the future of an avalanche. I wondered what sort of a brain was lodged above the eyes of Orton, the father.

"Go on," I encouraged him.

"There's nothing to it," said he. "Same old lingo you've heard a thousand times before, I guess. He's packed full of ambition for me. He herded me through high school, and he sure had his hands full doing it!"

I could imagine that. I pitied the school which had existed with a firebrand like this in its midst.

"Four years?" I asked.

"With a couple of breaks," said he. "I busted away a couple of times, but each time the old man came out and nabbed me and got me back. I missed six months each time.

"All the while the old man was talking law at me," went on Dick. "Yep, he never missed a chance. When he was starving back in the big town, he used to go to sleep dreaming about the lawyers that get to be presidents and senators, and the like! So he's got it planned for me. I'm to step right out and get to where he wanted to be. Sure, I waded through the Latin and all that bunk.

"He used to think it was great. He'd sit back and listen to me conjugate a Latin verb like he was hearing soft music; and when I busted out with some French, you would have thought that I'd handed him a shot of redeye—he's that far gone on education!"

"Good for him!" said I, thinking of Father McGuire and all of his patient hours spent to teach me the little that I had learned.

"Hey, Porfilo, are you kidding me?"

"Go on," said I. "I'm listening."

"It's pretty silly. The grand bust came when I was shoved into the debating team because they couldn't find anybody else to take the job in my last year at high school. The boys used to josh me quite a lot about being an orator. You see? It got my back up. I wrote up a line of lingo. I grabbed a-plenty of it out of books. Then I learned it by heart.

"When I was riding home at night, I used to spout out that stuff big and loud and talk so almighty fiery that I near scared my bronco to death. So when the time come for the debate itself, I wasn't fazed much by the crowd in the assembly room. Back yonder in the rear row was my old man. I took a slant at him, sitting up there looking white and nervous, as if I was on trial for murder.

" 'He thinks that I'm gunna bust down,' says I to myself. 'Here's where he gets one big treat.'

"So, when my turn comes, I sashay out and let the boys and girls have it.

"The others on the teams, they had been talking sort of strained and nervous, as if they was apologiz-

ing for being up there pretending to try to talk sense.
But I hit 'em from the hip. I pulled my punches
right out of the ground and talked like the folks in
that room was a measly crowd of mustangs, and I was
trying to herd 'em into the only corral where they belonged.

"They liked it. Now and then, while I was roarin'
and ragin' up and down the platform, I took a slant
at the old man and seen him turn from white to pink,
and then he begun to grin, and then he begun to
laugh, and then he begun to rub his hands and rock
around in his chair and nudge his friends in the ribs
and point out to them what a smart and sassy kid his
son was!

"I finished up in a blaze of glory and sat down
sweating, and pretty near to laughing, because they
give me quite a cheer, with the old man the leading
voice.

"After that debate there wasn't no doubt left in his
head. He figgered it out that his son was one of the
smartest men in the country, and was gunna walk
right through a governorship to the Senate and out
again to the president's chair. All he seen was visions
of me deliverin' an inaugural oration. All that he
prayed for was to live till the president could have
him to lunch in the White House.

"After that, he begun sort of talkin' up to me, like he
was a little boy, and I was an old man. He didn't give
no more orders to me. He just sat around and suggested things, and when I didn't do what he wanted,
he looked sort of sick and sad. He'd come in and sit
down and ask my advice about his business. Sure he
did. It would of flabbergasted you to see what a difference that debate of mine made to him—a lot of
lingo that I'd picked up out of the books and hung together with pins and paste, you might say.

"Well, I hadn't minded it so much in the days when he said that I was to be a lawyer and I said I wasn't, and then he roared out that he'd disinherit me, and give all of his money to charity—me being an only son! That wasn't so bad. It was just a fight.

"But when it got so that I said I wouldn't never be a lawyer, and he only turned white and bit his lip and looked down to his plate and stopped eatin'—why, then it sort of made me nervous. I felt that I was pretty near to doing what he wanted just because I pitied him.

"Finally things got pretty bad, and I seen that I'd have to bust loose.

"So I busted. The first thing that I done was to saddle a mule—because if a mule is good enough for Porfilo, it's good enough for me. I started out to show the old man that I wasn't the timber that they hacked lawyers out of. And here I am, Porfilo!"

## ··· 5 ···

I rode along for a while just chewing my lip and thinking not of the kid, but of poor old Orton who was living to see his son president.

"What do you want to do?" said I.

"Anything but be a lawyer."

"Want to be a rancher?"

"That's better."

"Interested in raising cows, eh?"

"Me? Not a bit."

"But you like riding the range, and working with a rope, and tail-ending cows out of tanks where they got bogged down and—"

"The devil, no!" said Dick. "I hate that sort of life! I never wasted the time to learn how to swing rope. It isn't cows that I want to play around with!"

"Just what *do* you want to be?"

"I figger on bein' free, the way that you are! Up here in the mountains—nothing to do but to ride around and have a good time."

"With what, Dick? You're the first man that ever rode two steps beside me in the mountains!"

"Why, if you ain't got men to play around with, you got the winds, ain't you?" he asked almost angrily. "If you got nothin' else, you got the danger of bein' caught, any minute! That's fun enough, by my way of thinking!"

I saw that I could not answer him immediately. But I knew that my heart bled for poor old Orton, somewhere in the hills of the cow-range country.

"How did your father get his start?" I asked.

"He got a little money together. He was sort of wild when he was a kid. That's why he hates wildness in me, maybe. He made some money selling newspapers, although it seems hard to believe that anybody could save money doing that, and then he floats out West. He worked on the range for a couple of years, just drifting around and learning the business, and liking the folks out this way and the way that they live.

"After all of that, he put his money—it was only a few thousand—into cows, and he settled down and got married and began to have luck. He's had luck ever since. He's boomed that little farm into a man-sized ranch, and it keeps growing. He's got a good head to be a rancher, the old man has! But why does everybody have to work?"

I remembered something Father McGuire said to me—that no man could be really happy except through work—but I was not so far gone that I would try salty maxims like that on a young fire-eater like Dick.

But you've no idea how old it made me feel to listen to him. Older than the hills!

We reached a good camping ground, and there I decided to stop for the night. Dick pointed out that it was fairly close to the Chisholm camp, but I felt that I was not apt to be followed quickly—not until they had been able to organize a sizable posse. Perhaps you will think that was vanity on my part, but one has to keep an eye on psychology as well as other facts. People in the mountains were afraid of me. I had come to count on that fear.

I told Dick to go ahead and make camp, because I intended to strike across country to see a man. I would not be back until the morning, I said; but I hoped to return at close to daybreak.

He did not like to have me go, but I persuaded him at last by giving him my word that I would be back and by leaving one of my guns. I pretended that I wanted him to look over the mechanism because it was beginning to be hard on the trigger. As a matter of fact, it worked more easily than I thought!

However, he was flattered to be asked an opinion. He made a little fire, and I left him sitting cross-legged beside it, working away at that gun with all his might.

Then I headed across country, and I made Roanoke work like mad. Because there was a good deal of emotion in me, just then, connected with that crazy youngster. Besides, I was utterly baffled, and I wanted to get to a wiser head than mine was.

I drifted over a bare, flat summit of piled rocks. A dozen big shadows started up before me and pitched over the other side down the side of the mountain— mountain sheep. They were gone, and the noise of their going ended, and the silence was suddenly and strongly upon me again before one could turn around —so to speak!

I peered over the ragged edge. It was a descent so frightful that even Roanoke would not have ventured it even had I the heart for such a risk. But these big creatures had gone down as though on wings. Suddenly I knew what was in the heart of Dick Orton. He wanted to be like those great sheep—wild and free and totally unhampered.

Well, I had read books—mostly poetry—where there is a great deal of talk about untrammeled freedom, but I have to confess that I have always found freedom a pretty painful thing—and the greatest bore in the world! We're made to help one another—or disturb one another. Here and there is a bad man or a worse woman; but on the whole, are not people a pretty reasonable lot?

For my part, I have not much sympathy with the fellows who spend a great part of their time hating others. I can state offhand that I've never come to know anyone without finding a great deal worth liking. That goes for a lot whom I started by hating with all my heart—my bitterest enemies, in fact.

This night, I pushed Roanoke hard, as I said before. The ordinary route would have cost us twenty-five or thirty miles of hard travel. I took the air-line route and landed where I wished to be in just half of that distance and about two hours of time. I left Roanoke grunting and mumbling to himself—a way he had when he felt that he had been worked too hard—and I waded through the forest and the undergrowth until I came to the back wall of a house with just a glinting high light on one window where a star left its image as though in water.

I went up to that window. It was half open, and so low to the ground that I could lean in and smell the warmth of the house and hear the breath of the sleeping man.

"Lawton!" said I.

There was no start or exclamation. Manhunters learn to waken smoothly and noiselessly as they learn to pull their guns. An instant more and he was in front of the window.

"Porfilo," I explained.

At that he grunted very loudly.

"You've come to tell me what a pretty party you've had, I suppose," said the sheriff. "You've come to tell me what the papers left out, I guess. You've come to tell me what fun it was to stand up there and drop three gents one after another—"

"Sheriff—" I tried to break in.

But he was too angry to listen to reason. He went on in full flood: "I want to tell you how much fun it was to have people cracking jokes about me—a sheriff that went up to get a pardon for a man that he wasn't able to catch.

" 'He's swore that he'll put his hands on Porfilo, and this is the only way that he can do it!'

"That's what they said about me!

"Well, Porfilo, it was a lot of fun to go to meet the governor the next morning after you'd held up the stage. Did you know that he was a cowpuncher when he was a kid?"

I said that I did not know it.

"He was a mule skinner, too," said the sheriff, "but the cussing that he done that morning laid over anything that I ever heard tell of from any mule skinner or cowpuncher that I ever seen! The cussing he done was worthy of a governor, I tell you—it was that rare. When he got through cussing, he turned around on me and Father McGuire and told us what he thought of us for having made a fool of him about a gent that had done what you had done."

"Sheriff," I protested, "I didn't stick up that stage."

He only snorted. "The holdup boy rode a mule and admitted to your name, you blockhead!"

"Lawton," said I, "I have four thousand dollars in my pocket which I can prove didn't come from that holdup. You know me. I ask you if I'd hold up a stage when I had that much cash in my wallet?"

It silenced him for a moment, but still he was not convinced. He had been so thoroughly humiliated at the governor's office that he could not swallow his grudge against me all in a moment.

"Who else *could* do it?" he asked.

"A fool kid, eighteen years old, who got tired of a quiet life, had read a lot of bunk about me, and started out to make news."

It struck the sheriff in a heap. It was so unexpected that he saw that I could not have invented it. Then I told him the story as I had heard it—briefly.

"What am I to do?" I asked.

"Shove a gun under his nose and bring him into town and collect the pardon of the governor the next day!" he declared.

"And send one of the best kids I ever met to prison for the best part of his life?"

The sheriff cursed most profanely.

"Well?" said I.

"Damnation!" said the sheriff. "Why d'you bring your soiled life around to me and ask me to launder it for you? Do your own dirty work!"

"I ask you, as a sheriff what would you do?"

He only groaned. Then, "You're right, Leon," said he.

"About what?" said I.

"You might have saved your long ride," said he. "Of course I wouldn't do nothing other than you're gunna do—and that's to give the kid a chance to make good! Now get out of here—I wish that I'd never heard your name, and never seen your face!"

I must add that there was another word from the sheriff as I disappeared—a final greeting which he leaned out the window to call after me as I hurried away through the night. I heard his voice—a little modified for fear lest some other person in the house might gather what he had to say:

"I'm on the warpath after you again, Lee! I'm coming hot-foot. The governor told me that I had to—or quit!"

I was sorry for Lawton. Of all the fine and fearless men who ever drew breath or buckled on guns, there was never a finer or a more fearless one than our sheriff. I loved him as I have rarely loved another man. All my association with him had been a strange one of friendship and of enmity, and I hardly knew what to say of him to myself, except that I had a lasting conviction that if the time ever came when he had me cornered and could put the irons on my wrists, he would wish heartily that it was another man besides himself who was doing it.

Yet it was his duty to hound me to the best of his ability. An ability which no one had dared to question until the long list of his failures to secure me after I had repeatedly broken the law in his own county!

However, I was rather downhearted after my interview with him. That he was right I did not doubt. It was what my own conscience told me. Though, perhaps, some fine quibblers might declare that the sheriff was wrong, and that he would encourage lawbreaking by such advice as he had given to me on that night, yet I was sure that he was right. For if Dick Orton were to be sent to the penitentiary, it would surely be the making of a real bad man when he came out.

I knew where the Orton place was, though I had never seen the owner, or heard him described until Dick described him that evening. I calculated that I could get to the Orton ranch by midnight, and that I could round back to the place where I had left Dick by the time that the morning dawned.

So I pressed Roanoke ahead. He had covered a frightful distance and raised and lowered his strong body a prodigious number of yards in the past twenty-four hours, but still there was something in him which responded. I am sure that no horse could have lived with him over half of the journey which he had made. But when he swung into his long trot, he ambled along with as little friction as a wolf.

At that trot I took him down the next ravine which opened over the heads of the rolling hills, and then across the hills to the Orton ranch. It was a typically ugly place. A long, squat building under the brow of a low northern hill. There was not a tree near it. Summer must have burned that house until it was an oven inside, and winter must have frozen it.

I left Roanoke at a little distance, as usual, and took the extra chance of loosening the girths so that he might breathe. Then I went straight to the front door and knocked loudly. There was finally a faint groan and the squeak of a footfall in an upper room. Then a head and white-clad shoulders leaned out.

"Word from Dick," I called softly.

There was an exclamation which did not form any words; the figure disappeared, and presently I saw a light flare behind that upper window. Voices muttered rapidly; then steps descended, and the door was thrown open. I saw a grizzly-headed man I knew must be Orton, and behind him the frightened face of a woman.

"Keep your light back!" I commanded, as he began to raise it above his head. "Send Mrs. Orton back. I'll talk to you alone. Do you understand?"

Mrs. Orton made some sort of an incoherent protest, but her husband, after a moment of thought, waved her back, and she hurried down the hall.

"Will you come in?" he asked me.

He put the lamp down on a hall table and then started violently with a little groan of consternation when the light fell dimly over my face. I have said that it was not a handsome face nor a pleasant one, and my blunt features were too well known through the mountains.

Too many posters had been published showing me and naming the reward upon my head—dead or alive! That was always the frightful part of it, to me. Dead or alive, as though I were already in part a corpse. At least, so far as the law cared for me!

"Porfilo!" breathed old Orton.

But his fear left him instantly. He was too full of a greater emotion than fear to let it control him for more than a moment.

"It's you, eh?" he went on bitterly. "Ah, I might of knowed how it was. It was you that got my boy away at last, Porfilo? Him after talkin' about you and dreamin' about you for three years! Now what more d'you want out of me?"

"A little common sense, and a little patience to hear what I have to say," said I.

He folded his arms and stared grimly at me. He was a big man, like his son, and he had his son's straight eyes, though they were covered with a dense gray brush of bristling hair.

"I'll hear you yap," said he.

"Dick is with me in the hills," said I.

"I guessed it."

"I've come to tell you that I want to get him back to you if I can."

"That's likely—having got him there once!"

"He got *himself* there," said I, growing a little hot.

"How, if you please?"

I was so angry that the words snapped out of their own accord.

"By holding up the Sanburn stage."

The old man blinked at me for a moment, and then in a flush of rage, he lifted his fist as though he would strike me to the floor for blasphemy.

"You blackguard!" cried he. "When you and your mule were seen there—and when you named yourself to 'em?"

"Was it likely that I'd name myself?" said I. "Did you have all of your mules the day after the holdup?"

He had framed an answer to the first question with his lips, but the second question apparently struck a chord in him, for he started and then lowered his hand.

"Porfilo," said he rather weakly, "what does it mean? Will you try to tell me?"

"He played the fool," said I, "because you've talked him almost mad with this law stuff. He wanted to prove that he was fitted for something else—and he's proved it, right enough. With three men in bed on account of the proof!"

Something in the way in which I said this—for truth sometimes is as piercing as the sound of a gong—dropped him weakly into a chair and opened his eyes at me.

"I don't want to hurt you too much," said I, "but I came here tonight to tell you where Dick is, because I know that you must be almost mad."

"Aye," said he in a broken voice. "Almost mad these last days. I thought—he was dead!"

"He's very much alive. As I said before, I'm going to try to get him back here to you. When I send him, I'm going to try to have him in a mood to listen to reason. I'm going to try to have him in a mood to do whatever you want him to do. Even law school, if you can't think of a better thing!"

"Porfilo," said he, "you talk like a white man. Only, my head is sort of spinning. I don't see—"

"He's big and husky, and you've let him have an easy life," said I, "so that he doesn't like the idea of work. That's the whole of it."

"He's had an easy life," admitted Orton.

"He doesn't want work of *any* kind. He thinks that outlawry is a sort of second heaven. He's been envying me for the way in which I've lived in the mountains."

"Aye, I know that."

"Before I'm through with him, I want to teach him that it's pretty far from a rosy dream. You understand? I want to send him back with his wings clipped. But that leaves one thing more."

"The stage robbery!" groaned Orton.

"Which is the one thing that stood between me and the governor's pardon. Now, Orton, if I let your boy know what that freak of his cost me, do you know what he'd do?"

"Ride down and deliver himself up!"

"Exactly."

The rancher gripped his hands together and bowed his head.

"The one way out, Orton, is to fix the people who were in that stagecoach so that they won't testify against him when he *does* give himself up."

"Fix them?"

"You could handle some of the men, I suppose, by simply telling them the truth about who did it and by paying back the money Dick took, and by paying their doctor bills. You could fix some of the cheap ones with a little money. A bit of persuasion of the same kind might smooth things over all around."

"Is there a chance?"

"The only one to keep either Dick or me from jail. I'll give him a fair chance. I'll tell no stories out of school. I'll see that when I send him back to you, he'll have all the holdup money with him. I promise you I'll not let him part with a cent of it. In the meantime, you work on your end of the deal—and remember that they've doubled the price on my head. So make it fast!"

The perspiration was fairly rolling down his face.

"Porfilo," he said, "if I say that—"

"I don't want thanks," said I briskly. "I want results. So long, sir!"

I stepped back into the night and then hurried off to find Roanoke.

## ··· 6 ···

Even that giant of a mule—with a heart as strong as his body—had had enough. There was something uncertain about his gait when he struck the mountains again, and I got down from the saddle and jogged along beside him.

So we struck away as well as we could, but I was falling far behind my established schedule, so that I knew, before long, that I could not possibly reach the camp of Dick at dawn.

Indeed, I was still a good two miles of rough country away when the sun came up in the east. I pressed on with a growing anxiety. I was worried as to what he might do, left to himself in the daylight.

Then, like an answer to my thought, I heard three shots from the exact direction of the camp, which was still a good mile away from me. The distance made the explosions dull and small, and even at that distance I knew that a revolver was speaking, since there is a metal clanging in the sound of a rifle.

Those noises were made by my new friend, Dick Orton. Even that rash head of his would not permit him to shoot a revolver for the mere pleasure of target practice. No, perhaps even that folly would be possible in him, near though we still were to the camp of Chisholm.

At any rate, there was need for me to hurry. Roanoke had recovered something of his strength, due to my long run, and when I swung into the saddle he was able to take me up the slope at his long, swaying trot. We covered the next crest, and then we dipped through a lane of trees down the slope beyond.

We were about halfway down it and a scant half mile from Dick's camp where I had left him when Roanoke braced all four feet and slid to a halt. There he stood with his ugly head thrown high, sniffing danger. I, too, felt something like a shadow of apprehension pass over me. I snatched out a revolver and whirled in the saddle.

There, behind me, half hidden by a tree trunk, was the body of a man with an end of a flung rope in his hand. I saw, but I saw too late, for at the same instant, with a fatal whisper in my ear, the noose dropped over my head and then bit hard around my body and imprisoned both arms at the elbows against my ribs; then came the tug of the rope thrower's full weight, and I was dragged clumsily, helplessly, from the saddle and so, with a stunning thud, fell at full length upon the ground.

It has taken some time to tell of this. But my first glimpse of the thrower was the very instant that the rope dropped over my head and gripped my arms. From that moment I was helpless and lay bewildered, while the very trees around me turned into madmen!

Not two or three men, but a full score leaped out around me, shrieking their triumph at one another and beating backs, thumping shoulders—almost too delighted with themselves to go ahead with the simple task of securing my hands behind me.

They tied me as though my flesh were fire and would burn through ordinary bonds. They swathed me in thirty or forty pounds of rope, and still some of the older men seemed a little anxious. But I had no thought of attempting to escape.

I looked about me on the bedlam with a sort of detached interest. It did not seem possible that I, Leon Porfilo, of Mendez, the son of the town butcher, the pupil of Father McGuire, should have attained such a bad eminence that so many brave and strong men could go half hysterical at the thought of it.

The more serious portions were already making figures on the ground. There were twenty-one of them. How many times did twenty-one go into fifteen thousand?

About seven hundred bucks apiece!

"That ain't bad for a day's work," said someone.

"Something extra for Lefty!" three or four chimed in.

Lefty came blushingly forward, a long-shinned, gray-headed cowpuncher—the same who had caught me in the noose of the rope.

"Aw," said Lefty, "I ain't got a claim to two shares. Anybody could of—"

"Don't believe it," I put in here. "It took an expert to get that rope through the air without a swish that would have scared a whole herd of buffaloes. I congratulate you!"

Here all other voices ceased, and they stared at me. They had treated me before that moment as though I were a beast in ropes, or a demon in a bottle—a thing to be gaped at, but only with horror. They seemed to see something human in me after that.

"How did you manage to make your throw so quickly after Roanoke stopped?" I asked him.

"I seen him begin to slow a mite. So I started swayin' the rope. Just as he got toward a halt, I let her go. About a fifth of a second more, and you'd of drilled me, Porfilo."

He rubbed his chest as though he had a foretaste of where that bullet might have entered.

"I suppose I should," I admitted. "Who's in charge here?"

"Why, nobody," said someone.

I could not believe it, but it was the entire truth. They were simply a random lot of cowpunchers and lumbermen and hunters who, hearing the news of my appearance at Chisholm's camp, had gathered there to hear all that had happened. Then they had blundered up the mountainside the instant the sun rose in a vague hope that they might come on traces of me. Half of them were on foot!

Never was there such a blind and helpless beginning to a manhunt, and never a hunt that turned out more beautifully!

I had been riding in such a blind haste, with my eyes so fixed upon the higher side of the mountain, that I had not seen the telltale prints of the score of men and horses on the ground over which I rode. Well, I have always felt that this was fate.

Although, perhaps, a better explanation may be that long success had made me careless. Just as a man feels that he is invincible—at that very moment the ground is sure to be jerked from under his feet.

I have often been asked just how I felt at the moment of my capture. What terror and horror and despair welled up in me like shadowy waves. But I have to confess that I felt no great amount of any of those three emotions. Neither did my whole life flash before me; neither did I see the yawning gates of the prison.

I was a little frightened and a good deal irritated because I had made such a clumsy end after a rather stirring career; but nothing disturbed me as much as the ache of my bones from my fall.

After that, I think I was rather more amused than anything else, and very busy watching the faces around me and listening to their voices, and getting a cheap pleasure, I confess, out of the joy they felt in capturing me.

On the whole, I don't think that the actual hand of danger is ever so terrible. What breaks the heart and shatters the nerve is the face of danger in the distance. To wait for her approach is a frightful thing. But when she actually strikes, it is not much. I have heard men say that people in the mouth of a lion, gashed and broken by the tremendous jaws, feel no pain whatever. And danger is like a lion. She is most frightful in the distance.

At least, I am certain that when they lifted me to the back of Roanoke and tied my feet beneath his belly, I was not at all enraged with my captors. They were a very good-natured lot, all jovial and smiling, of course, because of that good morning's work which meant a year's pay popped into their pocket for a single half-day's outing.

Lefty was placed beside me, as the post of honor. The rest of them grouped themselves in convenient array to guard against an attempt at escape or a possible rescue. Far before, behind, and to either side they distributed flank, van, and rear guards to take heed of coming danger.

Then there was an inner cordon of five men, including Lefty, who rode around me, each with a gun in his hand, while the remaining nine formed a larger circle beyond these.

In this fashion I was brought down the slopes and back to the Chisholm camp.

Lefty was a very amiable host. He seemed to be rather ashamed of the part which he had played in the affair, and he kept insisting as he rode along at my side that he had no bad feelings toward me—that he wished me well—that he hardly knew why he had ridden out with the posse—and that he earnestly hoped that I would come well out of my trouble.

I could not help smiling at Lefty, but I knew that he meant what he said.

"But," I said to him, "it's too bad that you weren't alone. You would have had the fifteen thousand all for yourself!"

It was too large a sum for Lefty to grasp in one sweep of the eye; another idea startled him.

"Porfilo," said he, "d'you think that I'd of tackled you if I'd been alone? Not in a million years; I ain't such a fool!"

If I had protested, he would have said a good deal more, but I made no answer to him. However, the truth is perfectly patent that, no matter how many there were around Lefty, it was he and he alone who captured me. When I looked at his simple, good-natured face, a great deal of the vanity left me.

So they brought me in to Sanburn, and they brought me in with a veritable army.

For the news had shot like magic across the mountains, and scores of hurrying riders were spurring to reach me; and in the midst of shouting and dust and snorting horses and jingling of bridle chains and spurs and thudding of hoofs, they escorted me into the town.

## ••• 7 •••

I had a sort of triumphal procession into the town, as one might say. That is, everyone came to windows and waved at me and shouted, and I smiled back at them. In fact, I felt no malice. I was only glad that the long fight was over and that I no longer had to freeze and starve on the mountains and live shut away from my fellows.

That is what I felt, I should say, as I passed through the streets of the town, but the moment the doors of the jail closed behind me and sent a long iron clangor through the big empty space within, my pleasure ended. I cast one side glance at Lefty, and Lefty, having met that look, fell suddenly into the background. From that day to this, I have never seen his face!

After that, I was prepared for what they did. First they tried me with questions, to which I refused all answers, except to admit that my name was Leon Porfilo. There was no use dodging that; but for the rest they got nothing from me. Then they dressed me for the cell.

They left me my clothes, but those clothes were wrecked before they were through. They searched every nook and cranny where so much as a needle could be hidden. They probed and reprobed my shoes, and even investigated the sections of which the heels were built, for fear lest I might have something concealed there—some tiny instrument with which I might unlock my bonds and escape.

In the same fashion they went over all my clothes. It took three men a patient hour of searching before they were sure that my clothes did not contain hidden secrets, and even when that search had ended, they did not appear entirely certain that all was well, and they watched me with extremely wistful eyes.

Next they led me to the cell and put on the irons. Heavy irons for the wrists, but with a mercifully long chain connecting the bracelets, and ponderous irons for the feet, hitched to a great ball. It was possible for me to move across the floor at a snail's pace, dragging that impediment behind me, but I made as much noise as a cavalry charge when I *did* move. They were shameful things, those irons, but they were very effective. I have often wondered why that old-fashioned stuff is not more often used. There would be fewer escapes, by far!

There I sat or lay or stood in Sanburn jail for ten mortal days. There I waited, and the crowds filed past the bars every day and pointed and whispered and laughed and gaped at me.

"There is Leon Porfilo!"

They were never weary of filing by. At first I could not endure their glances and my sense of shame, but afterward I schooled myself, and I used to sit back and smoke a cigarette and watch them, and meet every eye in turn. It was very odd.

There is a weight in a steady glance that some people cannot endure. Most of those who went by those bars could not endure my stare. The men, particularly. Their eagerness went out; more than one of them would actually look the other way, with a shudder. I think that they felt I was trying to jot down their faces for future reference, so that I could take revenge upon them for my shame! The women were bolder, strange to say.

Western women do not fear men. These girls and ladies looked at me with horror, sometimes, but more often with pity, and still more often with a sort of smiling good fellowship, for all the world as though they understood exactly what had brought me there, and it was no fault with which they could not sympathize.

But it was a bitter grind—to endure those straining eyes day by day. Yet the days were heaven compared with the frightful, black, hopeless nights. No, not black, either, for from a far corner of the cell room a single lamp cast a vague glimmer, and there was never a time when I could not make out the faintly gleaming parallel bars which confined me, and beyond them more dim lines of light—a forest of steel.

Sometimes I felt like running at those bars and tearing at them with my hands. I fought that feeling back —always with a horrible thought that someday the temptation might be too great for me. If I slipped into madness once, where would I end?

For I had lived for three years and a half on the mountains as free as a bird, and the cold and the wretchedness which had been driving me back toward other men were now forgotten. All I could remember was that to be free is to be glorious. I yearned for the regions above timberline—and for Roanoke! The ugly head of that mule drifted across my dreams like the symbolic eagle of my country.

It was not always a drifting line of people who paused, and gaped, and went on—men, women, and children who were lifted to gaze at me and learn that bad men came to such an end as this. For now and then the line ended. It was restricted to calling hours, you might say. In between people of importance were allowed to come to visit me. The newspaper reporters were always considered people of importance!

Well, I tried to tell myself that such fellows were beneath my attention. But they weren't. No one is beneath the opinion of any man. What the beggar in the street thinks, troubles the mind of the king. There's no doubt of that. I smile at the rugged people who damn all the world except a few friends. Margaret O'Rourke came to me, too, and I dragged my iron ball across the floor, making a small thunder behind me, and took her small hand through the bars. She did not speak half a dozen words, and those were incoherent. She came in trying to be brisk and cheerful, like her old self. But she began to cry at once, and clung to the bars and buried her face in her arm and wept like a child.

Then I saw, all at once, that I had treated her not as a man should treat the woman he loves, but like a sulky fool. I despised myself. I saw in Mike the truth of her, which was all womanly and gentle.

Her visit and one other were the only ones that did me good.

The other visit was from Father McGuire. I had not seen him for years. But he looked the same. A little older and more tired, but not much. He was full of impatience and could hardly pause to shake my hand.

Then he wagged a lean forefinger at me. "Leon Porfilo," said he, "you did not hold up that stage!"

"Of course not," said I.

"There is not much careless brutality in you. Besides—you would not tell your name—and more than that, if you had been there, really, I don't think that any guns would have been pulled against you! Now I'm going back to see that governor—although I've tantalized him about you until he hates my face. Only this much before I go:

"Keep your head high and your hands clean—as clean as you've kept them up to this time, my boy! I know what you are; and a few others guess what you are. We need you back on our sides. Good-by!"

The world is not large enough to hold two like Father McGuire!

That same day, a little withered man stood in front of the bars and smoked a cigarette and looked me up and down. It was Tex Cummins, who had freed me from the jail in Mendez three years before—freed me because he thought he could use me afterward.

"Well, well, Leon," said he, "I see that you're back to your old tricks again—popping yourself into free lodgings!"

I did not answer him. I knew that I had not sufficient subtlety of tongue to talk with such a man as Cummins.

"But in the meantime," said he, "I wonder if it is not just as well that you are in here instead of out there!" He waved his hand to indicate the outer world. "Because out there, I was coming close on your trail, my lad, and if I ever catch you—you will wish that you had taken a shorter cut to purgatory, Porfilo."

I had to make an answer to that. So I dipped up a little of the bitterness and the scorn that was in me and I said to him: "I've beaten you and your crowd before, Cummins, and I'll beat you again. I'll tell you why: A crook has no real chance against an honest man!"

He laughed in an ugly way.

"Well, honest man," said he, "here's your reward. But if you'd worked with me, you fool, you'd be rich and happy now, Porfilo."

That was the way he left me. But I am glad to say that he did not make me regret.

Now I come to that tenth day of my stay in the prison, which was one of the strange days of my life. I had felt that I was almost at the end of my nerve strength, and I said so to Sheriff Lawton, who came in for the first time.

He told me that the string of visitors who came to gape at me would be shut out from that time forward, and he heartily damned the keepers who had allowed them to come in to me up to that time.

When he questioned me about the stage holdup, I had to admit that I did not care to talk of that affair, and my reluctance angered him a great deal.

"I believe you," he said. "I believe that you didn't do that job. It doesn't ring like Porfilo to me. Stage stick-ups are a little too spectacular for your particular kind of nerve. But, Leon, how the devil am I to base my belief on anything more than a mere hunch? What the devil will a jury say?"

"Juries will give me no sort of a show anyway," said I. "How can they give a show to a man with fifteen thousand on his head?"

Lawton grinned sourly at me. "They've collected their reward," said he. "Well, I'm glad that I didn't have a share in it, boy!"

I thanked him for that, and he talked cheerfully, but about other things, until he left me.

After that, a long, long day followed. From one small, high-placed window on the wall, a spot of sunlight was cast upon the floor. Far slower than the movement of the hour hand of a clock, it seemed to me, that spot of sun crept to my cell. When it reached me, I kneeled and held out my hands to it until my fingers were yellowed and warmed by it. It was more than washing in liquid gold to me, at that moment!

But, after the spot of sun had left the floor of the cell nest, the long evening began. It was an age while the soft light of the end of the day deepened from yellow to rose, and then to violet outside the window. I stared at the window frame as though it were my last hope of life.

Through it there seeped in a faint tang of the alkali dust which was raised by playing children and by passing riders in the street. Never was such a sweet perfume! Through the window, also, came fragments and rhythms of pleasant voices. Oh, who has not noticed that all voices are pleasant so long as they come from human lips and from the distance?

I felt myself growing weaker. I had a queer choking in my throat and a lightness in my head. I knew that my nerve was breaking down. But then the sorrow of the day turned into the black bitterness of the night!

I thought of the pure, cold winds that comb the upper mountains where I had lived so long, and the last bird voices in the wind, and the bell tones of lowing cattle out of the valleys—the deepening dark and the sudden nearness of the stars above my head.

Yes, I was weakening fast. If someone had entered the door of my cell at that moment and exclaimed: "Porfilo, what are the sins and shameful actions of your life?" I should have confessed them all swiftly, almost eagerly!

Western towns fall asleep early, just as they rise early. Now all of Sanburn was lost in silence. Not perfect silence, but that deeper stillness through which occasional noises burst on the ear with a sudden violence —a dog barking, a sharp break of laughter, an oath from a passing man. But even these sounds grew less frequent. Sanburn slept.

But I did not sleep. For two days and nights I had not slept, and I lay on my cot with a thudding heart-beat, telling myself that another night of torture was about to begin, and that when the morning came, if I had not slept, I should be close to hysterical weakness —close to a tearful breakdown. I—Leon Porfilo!"

I had always looked upon myself as a creature made out of some stubborn material, as different from the stuff that composes other men as iron and rock are from wood. But now I had a brief inner glance, and what I saw astonished me.

That night wore past its first few ages, and then I heard the guard, who had been rustling a newspaper in the outer office, begin to walk up and down the floor. There was a wooden floor out there—a concrete floor in the cell nest, to embed the lower end of the bars. Every creak of the floor was very audible to me. Once he opened the door and came in to me.

"Hello, Porfilo!"

I did not speak.

"Sulky still!" snarled the guard.

I think he had been drinking a bit. There was a thick, numb articulation in his speech. For that matter, it is no cheerful task to be night guard in a jail.

"Good night," said I.

"It ain't no easier on me than it is on you," he declared. "Why not loosen up a bit and act sort of human? I ain't a wolf, Porfilo. We could help each other waste a little time."

I did not reply. It made me sick at heart to even think of chatting with my prison keeper. So he turned on his heel with an oath, and was off again. The door closed heavily on him; his pacing up and down the office floor began once more.

Then his striding paused. I heard the opening of a door and then, distinctly, a gasping noise, a scuffle—after which the outer door of the jail closed heavily.

Another pause—a muffled voice—and the office door was flung open. I saw the guard come hurrying, the lantern in his hand. Behind him stalked a tall fellow. A sway of the lantern and the upfling of the light struck across a masked face.

"A lynching party!" I thought, and my stomach cleaved to my backbone.

But there was no murmur outside. Lynching parties do not gather so soundlessly. After all, my crimes were not of the variety which induce lynching.

The keeper paused at my door, unlocked it, and stepped in.

"Take your time," said the masked man. "There's no hurry."

It was a deepened, roughened voice, but I knew it—Dick Orton! Suddenly a great spring of joy opened in my heart. A wine of happiness rushed through me. I loved Dick Orton. I loved the whole human race for his sake!

The keeper had seen or heard enough to throw him into a panic. His hands were trembling, but he managed to find the locks and to turn the key in them. The shackles fell from my hands. I clasped my numbed wrists and chafed them. The weights fell from my legs—I stretched myself on tiptoe, turned suddenly lighter and stronger than ever I had been before.

"You," said Orton to the keeper, "stand back in that corner. If you yap, I'll come back and blow your brains out."

He drew me out of the cell and closed the self-locking door on the guard. Then he thrust a pair of guns into my hands. I slipped them in my pockets, however.

"Why?" Dick paused to ask me.

"It's never worth a killing," said I.

He merely grunted, and then he led the way through the cell room. At the office door he paused. Behind us there was a muffled sound—the groan of the guard in shame and in despair!

We stepped into the office.

"There's a rifle," said Dick. "Do you want it?"

I took it from the wall. There is nothing much better than a rifle by way of a club. Then I followed Dick calmly through the front door, first cramming on my head the sheriff's own old sombrero which hung from a nail.

Two horses were tethered at the hitching rack. I saw that they were tall and well made. We untied them and swung into the saddle just as half a dozen punchers came rollicking around the bend in the street and swept by us.

One of them drew rein. The others slowed.

"Where you two been?"

"Trying to see Porfilo. They turned us down!" I laughed.

It was easy to laugh. Now that I was so close to freedom, I felt that a hundred giants could not have recaptured me.

The six laughed, also.

"We tried the same thing today. Lawton has shut down. The tightwad!"

Here a raging voice from the jail cried: "Help!"

"What the devil!" cried I. "What's up in the jail?"

"Help! He's gone!"

"An escape—Porfilo!" I yelled. I pretended to start for the jail door.

All the six were before me. With Indian yells they

lunged from their horses and sprinted for the front doors of the jail. Orton and I snapped into our saddles and turned the corner of the street.

Behind us was a confusion of sounds. In the street around us, and staring out from their doors and their verandas were men roused by the shouting from the jail—everyone with a gun. But they did not heed us, jogging slowly along. Oh, it was easy to be calm out of the cursed shadow of the jail!

We turned another corner and now the nerves of Dick Orton could stand the strain no longer. He gave his horse the spurs and we flew out of Sanburn at a raging gallop.

We flew out onto the dark hills beyond, with the wind of our gallop in our teeth and the clear, pure stars above us, reaching down to us, and the great, free mountains looming up into the sky on every side. I threw out my arms to it and thanked heaven for such a man as Dick Orton and for liberty.

Then we rode on. The confusion in Sanburn died behind us. We drew rein of one accord, without any spoken word. I reached for Dick's hand and found and crushed it.

That is the true story of the jail delivery at Sanburn about which the newspapers stormed and fought for so many days. Everyone said "Bribery!" and the jail guard left that section of the country, a disgraced man. But there was no bribery.

The thing had succeeded so simply because everyone expected that the attempt to escape would come from within, not from without. It was believed that I had no friend in the world except a sheriff and a priest. Sheriffs and priests do not break into jails!

## ··· 8 ···

"And Roanoke?" said Dick, after we had ridden for some time.

"Ah! If only I were on the back of Roanoke," said I. "Then the ride to freedom would be perfect. But perhaps it is enough that I am free, Dick. Free, free, free! I never knew what was in that word before!"

"It was easy," said Dick Orton rather thoughtfully. "Mighty easy."

"Easy for the man with the right amount of nerve, Orton. But I should have hesitated a good deal, even for my best friend."

"Would you?" said Dick, childishly pleased by that compliment. "But now you're just talkin'. Well, Porfilo, leastways we're on the move, and we're together!"

He said it grimly, as one who has accomplished a great thing. I really believe that to that foolish young-

ster it was a bit of heaven to be riding with me, simply
because the law had proscribed me, and men were
hunting me for a great price.

"It'll be twenty thousand after this," chuckled Dick,
and I knew that I was reading his thoughts correctly.

He could do nothing but chatter and sing, after that.
He told me how he had conceived the idea. After ten
days, he felt that they would begin to relax their precautions. Sanburn would be used to the sensation of
having such a prisoner in its midst. The guards would
be used to him, also.

So, that very evening, Dick had descended to his father's ranch and in the corral he had selected two of
the best horses—well-known and tried by him. These
he saddled from the harness shed and brought all
safely away.

But, before he went, he slipped up to the house in
order to play the spy and see what was going on there.
He had looked through the window of the living room
and seen enough to satisfy him—his mother and father, each screened behind a newspaper.

"The same as ever," said Dick, with a little of child-
ish chagrin. "I thought that they'd do a little grieving
about me!"

"You young fathead!" said I. "D'you think that
they're going to sit around and hold their hands and
cry about you for two whole weeks? Besides, maybe
they've found out that they don't need you as much as
they thought they did. The doctors cut out meat, and
they find that they can still get fat on vegetables!"

He did not take my banter in a very light manner.
He mused for some time, heavily, on this subject, and
muttered a few words to himself, but I was rather glad
to see that he was impressed. He had been an only
child and a favored child all his life—and even the

most manly fellow is apt to begin to take things for granted after a time.

I headed toward a house which I knew well. I had stopped there half a dozen times two years before, and I had been able to pay the squatter well for his trouble. He was a dark-faced Spaniard or Frenchman—I don't know which! But he had a foreign accent in his lingo that made me know that he was an outsider. You understand that I'm saying all of these things colloquially.

Well, I suppose that Joe Loveng was what generally went by the name of a "dago." Out West that means some fellow with a bit of Latin blood and black eyes and a swarthy skin and a language which leaves a taint in his English. That was the way with Joe Loveng.

Other punchers had little use for him. He was hard-headed. He ran sheep. His fist was tight. And—he talked queer. That is to say, he did not speak the particular sort of ungrammatical slang which was chattered in that part of the range.

He made his living, as I have said, by running a few sheep on his land. It was not very good land, but he made the best of it. He lost practically no sheep because he tended them as if they were his children, and he always had mutton that weighed twenty or thirty pounds more on the hoof than any other mutton on the range. When other sheep began to get pot-bellied and thin-backed, Joe's flock was as round as butterballs.

Besides, he had a little apple orchard which was in a hollow of rich ground, and he made cider from these and peddled the stuff when it was hard. He had a vineyard, too, rambling over a few hillsides where the soil was gravelly. Those vines gave him grapes enough to make several fine casks of wine every year, and that wine was famous all over the range. Even with these sources of income, Joe was never too prosperous—or at least he never showed his prosperity.

For one thing, whatever he produced, he had eight mouths to maintain. His own, his wife's, and six children, of whom the oldest was a fifteen-year-old girl when I last saw her. Since that time, two years before, I understood that Mary and several of her brothers had grown enough to be worked in the fields, and Joe Loveng was growing prosperous on account of the extra hands which he did not have to hire.

That was the family to which I was taking Dick Orton, and I told him about the place and the people as we went along.

It was a great game for Dick. He had never stayed in the company of an outlaw at such a house.

"But," said I, "there's one danger. If Joe should take it into his head to let it be known that you were seen at his house in my company—"

"He'd be pinched for taking in an outlaw—no matter who was with you!"

"Not a bit," said I. "He'd just explain that he was afraid of being killed if he did not entertain us."

"The coward!" said Dick.

"However," said I, "I think that Joe knows what side his bread is buttered on too well for that. He used to make good money out of me."

"No dago has a thought bigger than a dollar," declared Dick.

I was half inclined to agree with him, which shows that my education in the world was almost as limited as his!

We hove in sight of the twinkling lights of the house of Joe Loveng. It was eleven o'clock or later. We had ridden a full two hours from Sanburn, and I felt that by this time we had gone far enough to avoid pursuit.

Besides, after the first great rapture of freedom and the taste of the night air was out of my throat, I began to ache with weariness. This was the third night in which I had not closed my eyes, and for ten days every nerve in my body had been under a terrible strain.

My plan was to remain at Joe Loveng's and have a fine sleep until just before the break of day. Joe was one who never allowed the sun to see him in his bed, and therefore he would be able to waken us in time. After that, we could have a bite of cold breakfast, and then we would wing away into the gray of the dawn with very little probability that any of the scouts of Sanburn might come in sight of us. Even if we did, as a matter of fact, take a glimpse of them, we and our horses would be fresh and they would be fagged from a night of hard riding.

I confided all of this plan to my companion, and he agreed with it heartily.

Then he burst out into a great tirade of self-denunciation.

"Porfilo," said he, "if it hadn't been for me, you'd be a free man with the governor's pardon in your pocket, able to sass back every sheriff on the range, and as it is, you've got to run like a scared coyote and take to the hills!"

It made me rather gloomy to hear him talk in this manner. I had not realized that he would think the thing over so logically, and come to such a conclusion.

So we hove up to the door of Joe Loveng's house, and I leaned from the saddle and through the window pointed out the scene to Dick. There sat Joe Loveng, with his feet in slippers and his fat legs spread out to the warmth of the stove, and around him sat his flock of seven with their brown faces and their bright, black eyes which were never still. It was a pleasant sight.

But, "Holy smoke!" breathed Dick. "Look at that girl! Is that the reason why you want to come here?"

I looked again. It was Mary, sitting facing us. Between fifteen and seventeen she had turned from a child into a woman, and a lovely woman at that!

## ··· 9 ···

If I had had doubts as to whether or not Joe Loveng would remember me, they disappeared the instant that I met him at his door. He put out both hands and pulled me by the shoulders into the house. He kept one hand upon my arm; with the other he reached Dick Orton and pulled him in after me. And all the time he kept saying: "Meester Porfilo!"

But I cannot imitate his lingo. His words came up with a bubbling sound in the throat. He talked like a man who has just eaten some oily thing. He sent two of his oldest boys scurrying out to put up our horses. I wondered if it were the kind memory of me that caused this enthusiasm of Joe's, or the kinder memory of the last twenty dollars which I had left with him.

"Food—wine, Mary!" he snapped at his girl.

She was already at the kitchen door and whirled to smile back at us. I saw the flash of her white teeth, and her black eyes go through and through Dick Orton.

We sat down by the fire. Dick was very quiet, thoughtful, and kept observing all in the room with a reflective eye. He looked upon Joe Loveng's younger children, sitting in a bright-eyed, silent semicircle in the corner of the room. Dick Orton smiled upon them.

After that I began to worry.

In the meantime, Joe Loveng was hoping that the reason I was out of jail was because I had the governor's pardon. I could not help telling him that it was because I had something better than a governor's pardon—a friend. At this, Joe nodded and smiled at Dick, and Dick smiled back rather complacently. Then Mary came in with fried eggs and bacon and coffee and a pitcher of wine.

We marched through those provisions like lightning. I was busy eating and talking to Joe Loveng. Dick Orton said not a word, but he used his eyes very busily still, and when I announced that it was bedtime, and we got up from the table, I saw Mary Loveng blushing in the corner of the room.

There were two little attic rooms, and Loveng had his youngsters roll down our blankets there; I said good night to Dick and, drugged and sick with weariness, I blew out my light and turned in. All that I noted, through the window as the darkness flowed in around me, was the white face of a half moon which was riding in the eastern sky. Then I was asleep as suddenly as though I had been struck heavily over the head.

It seemed only an instant later that a hand seized upon my shoulder and the excited voice of Joe Loveng was barking at my ear:

"Meester Porfilo!"

I gathered my senses and both my guns and sat up with a jerk.

"Meester Orton, he has raised the devil!"

I blundered downstairs behind Joe Loveng and in the living room beneath, I found Mary cowering in a corner while Dick Orton marched magnificently up and down before her, like a lion before a lamb.

Loveng told the story with much heat. He had wakened at his usual early hour and struck the door of Mary, expecting her to start down at once to cook breakfast. But there was no answer. He opened her door and looked into her empty room!

Then, bewildered, he had gone to the window, and, looking down, he had seen them seated on a rustic bench beneath an apple tree, and each in the arms of the other. He had rushed down upon them, but when he appeared, Dick Orton had risen and declared that he would step upon Joe Loveng and make him pop with a loud noise—or something to that effect.

Here Dick put in simply that Loveng had drawn a knife on him, and then he had threatened to wring Mr. Loveng's neck if he did not get out of the way. As for the picture upon which Loveng had looked— why, it was very simple. Dick had not been sleepy.

He had lain in his blankets for a time—thinking! Then he had got up and slipped downstairs. When he stepped from the front door of the house, he heard a rustle of a figure disappearing around the corner of the house.

He, Dick, had gone out merely to smoke a ciga- rette, but now he saw that he might have the pleasure of apprehending thieves about to plunder the house of his host. He turned that corner and in a single bound he had apprehended—Mary Loveng herself!

Dick was very intense and serious about it. He paid no heed to the fury of Joe, but kept his eyes fixed upon me so gravely that I knew that he was telling the truth, and all the truth. Yet it was so foolish that I could hardly keep from smiling—which would have ruined everything.

It seemed that Mary Loveng, like Dick, for some mysterious reason, had not been able to sleep. She, too, had thought of a walk under the stars as a sedative before she tried to close her eyes. Therefore she had gone down—and been terribly frightened at the appearance of a man, suddenly.

However, when they discovered one another, they were rather glad of company. They simply sat down to have a chat. The air of that summer night was warm. It was very pleasant out under the stars to watch the way of the moon, diving through the silver clouds and putting them aside as the bow of a ship puts waves away.

They had remained there—simply in a friendly chat, talking about everything and nothing. Time had suddenly disappeared like a secret thief, and if they had still been sitting and talking when the morning broke—for yonder in the east there was now a thin penciling of gray—they really had no idea how so many hours could have jumped into a pocket. It was quite startling really!

I had not had a great deal of experience in such affairs, but one doesn't need experience. In certain important matters one is born with an instinct which is worth every whit as much as educated brains—no more! These two young idiots—their combined ages would not have added up to the age of good sense—had simply been thrown into a whirl at the sight of one another.

He was spectacular enough to have turned the head of almost any girl, and certainly she was a flashing pretty thing. So they had sat there all night, with never a wrong thought in their heads; and even now they were sick and white with love.

I never could understand why it is that love affects people in that way. Nothing gives folks a more distressed look—unless it is seasickness.

It was perfectly patent to me that Dick had spoken the entire truth. I asked him point-blank with a single stern glance, and his reply was a look as steady as iron. By that I knew, as well as though he had sworn it.

It was far other with Joe Loveng. He had listened to the story with a raging impatience. Half a dozen times I had been forced to put a hand on his shoulder to keep him from breaking in. But, when he had his chance, he broke into a violent explosion of foreign language that rattled out as fast as cobblestones rattle under the iron rim of a cart wheel.

What he said, of course, I had not the slightest idea. But suddenly Mary leaped up with a little cry and ran and clung to Dick. He, like a stalwart young jackass, put his arm around her and threw back his head—a very fine attitude and good enough to be tried in front of any camera. But it almost got him stabbed.

Joe Loveng whipped out a nasty-looking knife, almost long enough to have spitted them both, and I really think that he would have cut the throats of the pair of them if he had had his way. As for Dick, his gun hand was frozen around the girl; I was barely in time to get the wrist of Loveng and put a grip on it that made him drop the knife with a groan. I jammed my heel on the blade and sent it to splinters of flying steel. I was angry, too.

For I hate a knife. I think I like poison more than I like a knife. In the old days in Mendez I had learned to use one. A boy will practice any art of murder because he feels it brings him closer to the possibilities of manhood.

But, since my boyhood, I had come to detest bare steel. The very thought of it, to this day, edges my nerves and runs a sharp bit of ice down my backbone.

I said to Joe: "You're within an ace of getting your neck twisted off, you fool! What d'you mean by pulling a knife?"

Joe cowered for an instant and gave me an ugly side glance. Then his rage and his sorrow came hot in him again.

He declared that Orton had not told the truth— not half the truth. Dick swore that he had.

"Ah!" cried Joe Loveng. "Did you not kees her?"

"Say no!" whispered the white lips of Mary to her lover.

But he had become very grand and stately. "I did kiss her. Besides, she's gunna be my wife. Now, what've you got to say to that?"

What Joe had to say was a great deal. Part of it was in his own tongue, whatever that was, and the small moiety was in broken English. There was no difficulty in understanding, however. All that he had to offer was that if Mary attempted to marry such a man, he, Joe Loveng, would hang her with his own hands to the limb of the apple tree under which she had sat with her American lover.

That was rather rough talk, and I saw Dick Orton grow wild. I tried to catch his eye, but it couldn't be done. He stormed up to Joe Loveng and told him with a good deal of emphasis, helped out by a few curses which came right off the range, that if so much as a tip of her finger were hurt, if her feelings were in the slightest degree injured, he, Dick Orton, would return and take Joe Loveng by the nape of the neck and whittle him to the right size and put him into a frying pan and roast him, slowly.

This, or something to this general effect, was what Dick Orton managed to say through his teeth, fairly trembling with fury. But you cannot control such people as Joe Loveng with threats. I think that if I had been left alone with him, I could have smoothed out everything beautifully, but as it was, there was red blood in the eyes of Loveng before Dick had ended.

He ordered us out of the house, and I told Dick that we had better go hopping as fast as we could.

Nothing would do for Dick, however, but a finish in the grand manner. He had to sweep Mary into his arms and kiss her good-by in the presence of all of us. It was very silly, but it was rather touching, too. I didn't care a rap about Dick and his emotions. I knew that they would change quickly enough, and he would be well over his insanity.

But Mary was another matter. She clung to Dick and kissed him again and again, and vowed that she would die if he did not come back for her.

Well, they would have made a pretty picture if it had not been for the face of Joe in the background. He was a fire-breathing dragon, and no mistake!

I had to pry the lovers apart. Then I took Dick on one arm and with the other hand I gave Joe a twenty-dollar bill. He merely crumpled it in his palm and threw it in my face!

It was a pretty fair indication of how peevish he was. By this time I had worked up enough of a reputation—nine tenths of it totally undeserved—to keep most men from troubling me if they could avoid it, possibly. It was a bit of a shock to have that money thrown back in my face, but I let the matter drop. After all, I felt that we were too deeply in the wrong.

We went out to our horses and saddled them in a silence which lasted until we were well up the trail. Then Dick broke into song.

I am a fairly patient fellow, but that was too much. I drew rein and damned him heartily, from his hair to the tips of his toes, but Dick merely sang on, and raised his voice to drown me out.

"You have raised the devil!" I told him at last.

"It was a lark!" cried Dick Orton.

"May you burn for it!" muttered I. "You will if you dare go back to that girl."

"Dare to go back?" said Dick. "How can I dare to stay away—after I've promised her?"

That was the way with him. A worse thing to make a bad thing better. But after that I didn't attempt to argue with him. I would as soon have tried logic on a range bull.

## ··· 10 ···

My chief fear was concerning the wicked tongue of Joe Loveng, which could do Dick irreparable harm by publishing the fact that he was my companion in my flight and probably my rescuer. I had given Joe only one warning as I left, and that concerned silence.

Besides, no matter what Dick had done in the way of indiscretion, he had been guilty of no real crime. I determined that if Joe Loveng peached on Dick, I would make Joe an example never to be forgotten among mountain folks.

That was all for the future, however. For the present, I began as soon as the sun was high and warm to persuade Dick that he must turn back and leave me. He was as obstinate as Roanoke on a cold morning—than which I cannot imagine greater stubbornness. He insisted that he should accompany me—unless I really felt that he hampered me!

Hampered me? After he had dragged me from a

prison and while I was half mad for the lack of human company? I told him as much, but I begged him to go back to his home. I gathered together every reason on which I could lay my mind, and there were plenty of them, and all good enough to have convinced even a headstrong child. But Dick was worse than that. He was a headstrong man!

A dozen times I wished with all my heart that he had had my training under Father McGuire. It takes iron to break iron, and Father McGuire was finest steel. He had beaten me into shape of some sort when I was rather unmalleable stuff; he would have changed Dick even at his age.

However, the mischief having been done, there was nothing but to make the best of it, and that I determined to do. First of all, I wanted to drift my wild man away from the vicinity of Loveng's house. I succeeded very well in doing it. It was a full week later, and by keeping to the highlands—most of the time above timberline—I had been able to keep out of touch with trouble.

But then fate stepped into the ring and knocked my plans and my hopes galley west with a single punch.

I had to get word to the father of Dick—though he seemed to have forgotten that there was such a thing as a father and a mother grieving about him. So I decided that I must write a letter and get down to a town to slip it into a mailbox. Dick, of course, went with me. I could not take a step without having him along with me.

We got into a little crossroads town, and I found the box and I mailed my letter which told Mr. Orton that his son was still with me and that I was doing what I could to send him back, but that he was still obstinate. It was not much of a letter, but when I assured Orton that I was trying to keep Dick out of further mischief, I was rather assured that something good might come from it in the way of peace of mind for the old couple.

In the meantime, the pair of us were very keen to get news of the outer world. Seven days of wandering had been nothing to me, but they had made up seven years to Dick. It was he who got the paper—how, I don't know. It was an old paper—too old to suit me! For it was published five days before, and it bore in it in a first-page flare the very tidings which I most dreaded and had most hoped would not arrive.

For, on that page, there was printed a statement by Joe Loveng, which narrated how "the celebrated outlaw," Leon Porfilo, had come to his house and demanded his hospitality and received it—because he was afraid to refuse such a desperate character. Also, in the company of this man was none other than the son of the much respected rancher, Orton!

Dick Orton was furious at such duplicity on the part of Loveng, and I, myself, had a great desire to get at the man. But I needed only a moment of reflection to understand that Loveng had been hard tried by that experience with Dick.

"How far is it from here to Loveng's, do you think?" Dick asked me.

I saw what he was driving at at once.

"You'll not go back there, Dick," said I.

"And let Loveng have the run of me?" said Dick. "Nobody can stop me from going after him!"

I told him that I couldn't let him go, and I begged him to listen to reason. If he returned, it was very probable that the house of Loveng was being watched.

"What of that?" said Dick.

"You've thrown in your luck with me, and the world knows," I told him.

"What have I done, so far as they know? Why can't I go back to see Mary Loveng if I wish?"

"Go back to find her and all you'll see will be the inside of a jail!"

He was furious. He had taken the whole affair in such a casual way that he still could see no reason why the law should be at outs with him.

"This life of mine that you think so wonderful—well, Dick, you're seeing the true face of it now," I told him. "You can't go back to Loveng's place."

"I've got to," said he. "I've given my word."

"To whom?"

"To Mary."

"She'll be the last to want you to run into danger for her sake."

He was entirely bullheaded. Finally he turned his horse back on the trail and asked me if I would go with him or remain where I was.

At that, I rode in front of him and took hold of his bridle rein.

"Dick," said I, "I can't let you go. It's a crazy thing to do."

I should have known better than to take his rein. He was already so excited and so hot that it did not need much to put him quite off balance.

"Drop the rein, will you?" said he.

I did that at once and wished I had not touched it.

"Clear your horse from in front of me!" said Dick savagely.

I begged him to be reasonable.

"I'm not a kid!" thundered Dick. "I have a mind of my own, and I know how to use it! I'm going back to Loveng's. Keep clear of me, Porfilo!"

"You blockhead!" said I, getting a little too heated in my turn. "You shall not stir a foot that way."

"Who'll stop me?" asked Dick.

"I'll stop you if I have to!"

He was so angry that he sat on his horse trembling, for a moment.

"Porfilo," said he, "if you love your life, keep clean back from me!"

He tried to press forward. I kept my horse before him.

"Then, curse you, get your gun!" screamed Dick, and tore out his own Colt.

I was barely in reaching distance, and I was barely in time. I got his wrist just as the weapon came clear of the leather. The bullet went smashing at random against the face of a rock, and I threw my weight in at him.

The very first shock told me that I should have my hands full. He was a shade taller than I, but not quite so heavy. He had confessed that he had never done much work. But he was full of a natural strength.

The shock of our meeting tumbled both of us out of the saddles. We rolled under the bellies of the horses and then twisted apart for fear of their trampling hoofs. The moment I was away from him, I wanted the thing over.

"I've got enough, Dick," I yelled to him. "I don't want to fight!"

But he was entirely blinded with rage by this time. He came at me with a panther spring that I was barely able to dodge.

"Dick," I shouted to him, "I give up! I quit! I don't want to fight!"

I might as well have talked to a whirlwind. He came lunging again and got home a grazing blow on my temple that half dazed me and, worse than that, brought a flush of fighting heat into my own blood. It was a long time since I had had the joy of a personal struggle with another man, hand to hand. I jammed my left under the chin of Dick and hit him away from me.

There was enough force in that blow to make him gasp, but he was game to the core, and started back at me, smashing with both hands. He had some training, and he had a blinding turn of natural speed. But he had not yet stepped into his full power. Perhaps I felt as Andrew Chase felt, six years before, when he struck me to the ground.

"Take it, then!" I said to Dick, and slid my right over his shoulder until the knuckles fitted snugly along his jaw.

It pitched Dick squarely back upon his shoulders, and he did not rise again. It was a wicked blow; the jar of it had sent a tingle to my shoulder, and I was afraid that I might have broken the bone. But when I started to pick him up, he was already grunting and struggling.

He forced himself to his feet and began striking blindly toward me, quite out. There was no more force in his hands than in the hands of a child. I held his arms and begged him to steady up. He waved, and staggered for another instant. Then he shook his head violently, and his eyes were clear.

Through a very long moment we watched one another. I with my heart in my throat, for I was certain that I had lost one of the few friends I had ever made in the world. But, though there was rage in the eye of Dick, there was thought, also.

"You're too strong for me," he said huskily, at last.

"Dick—" I began.

But he broke in on me suddenly: "It was coming to me. It was coming to me, Porfilo. I see that, now. I'm glad that it came from *you*. I couldn't have taken it from any other man!"

"You slipped as you came in at me——" I tried to explain.

But he only grinned at me, a wry, mirthless sort of a grin.

"I understand all about it," said Dick, "I've had my licking. Well, maybe it will do me good!"

There are punishments of all kinds, but none that go much harder on a young man than the necessity of admitting that he has been beaten. When I heard my new friend Orton confess that he had been licked, I suddenly knew that he was twice the man that I had thought him before. I liked him twice as much.

He did not lose a penny's worth of pride, either. Altogether, it was an astonishing thing to me. For, when I had been licked the first and the greatest time in my life, I had blundered on until I was covered with bumps and blood. A priest had done the trick for me!

"Sit down over here, and let's think things over," said Dick.

We let our nags graze, and we sat down in the shade of a scrub oak—for we were in the lowlands at that time. He began to rub the crimson place where my knuckles had ground halfway to the jawbone.

"This is better than ten years of law," said Dick.

I said nothing. I was afraid that whatever I said would be too raw—too *much* to the point. Also, I was so astonished by the way in which he had taken the thing that I was fairly made mute by it. Can you think of striking a lion in the face and then seeing the brute lick your hand? There was a good deal of the lion in Dick.

I was only sure of one thing—that from that moment he was saved. The selfish boy would begin to die in him; he was a man. All in one stroke!

"I din't think that anyone in the world could do it," he told me. "Not even Leon Porfilo."

"A lucky punch—" I tried to begin.

He merely smiled. "I knew it the minute you got your grip on me. It was like having a ten-tined Jackson fork stuck in my flesh. I couldn't do a thing. I was like a kid in your hands. But now, Porfilo, the main thing is to make out what I should do next. I can't go blundering around trying to clean up the whole range. Somebody else will sap me in the same place—and not let me up when I go down!"

He laughed a little bitterly. "I thought I was a sort of a Hercules!" he said.

I let the poison work in him, because I saw that it was doing him a lot of good; but it was a pretty unpleasant thing to watch the pride and the good sense in him struggle together.

"There's only one right thing," I said at last.

"Tell me what that is?"

"Go back home, and face the music. See your father. Tell him that you've been playing the fool and that you want to do what he thinks is really best for you."

He answered me very indirectly.

"Why didn't you send a slug of lead through me, Porfilo, when I pulled my gun?"

I made no answer.

"Do you know what I would have done if I'd had the chance?" he went on. "I would of shot you down. That was how much temper was in me. I would of shot *you* down, Porfilo! Well, that's what makes me pretty sober now. Not the punch that knocked me out. That was nothing. But the stuff that was in my head just before you hit me. That's what makes me think!"

"Take it easy," I suggested.

"I am. I got only a quarter of what I deserved to get. You should be riding off, and I should be lying in the dirt, there, and looking at the sun, and never seeing it!"

He shuddered.

"Well," he said, "I'm going to do what you want!"

I found his hand and gripped it. "You're a fine kid, Dick," said I with all my heart in my voice.

He shook his head.

"But what about Mary Loveng—" said he.

"Well?" I asked, a little anxious.

"She had my promise to come back."

"She'll forget that."

He shrugged his big shoulders.

"I don't think so," said he. "I don't know. But we were pretty serious."

"Are you serious now?" said I.

"Me? That's not what counts. It's what might be inside of her head. That's what really counts, Porfilo!"

He could not have found a better way to silence me. Certainly this was a very different fellow from the Dick Orton of five minutes before.

"Think it out for yourself, Dick," I told him. "I can't help you now. Because you're not a kid anymore. You've turned into a man."

"I think I have. I want to forget the thing that I've been up to this time."

"Only remember that if you go to Loveng's house, you'll be running your head into a lot of trouble. Remember that Loveng will be waiting for you—and he won't be trusting to his own pair of hands. He'll have help, and plenty of it."

"I ought not to worry about the danger," he decided thoughtfully.

"Not for yourself. You have your father and your mother to think about," I suggested.

He shuddered a little at that. I think that for a moment he was about to give up the entire idea, but it came back on him.

"I agree to that," said Dick Orton. "I've got to think about them, and I shall—from this minute on! But before I go back to them, I have to have clean hands. My hands aren't clean until I've talked to Mary once more."

"Do you think," said I, "that one talk has been enough to fix her for life?"

"I thought so before," said he. "But I'm not quite so fat-headed now. Maybe she's forgotten all about me."

"What do you hope?"

"God knows that I hope she has!"

"I'm glad of that! I thought your head was pretty well turned, for a while."

"It was. But since you knocked some sense into me —well, I've been seeing only one thing when I think of her, and what I've been seeing is not her pretty face."

He paused again and frowned at the ground. It was a sad thing to watch the boy die out of him and the man take its place.

"Only her hands, Porfilo," he murmured. "That's what I'm seeing now. Big, broad, stumpy, calloused hands—like the hands of a man. Confound it, I know that she got those hands by doing good, honest work in the fields, and yet—"

"Good, honest work—and she's a good, honest girl," I reminded him.

"I'm thinking of that," he declared. "Yet—it makes a mighty lot of difference, Porfilo. You understand, don't you?"

"I'm keeping out of it. It's up to you and your conscience, Dick."

At this, he sighed. "Conscience is the devil!" exclaimed he. "Particularly when it's a stranger to you!"

"You've never seen its face before?" I chuckled.

"Never!" grinned Dick Orton. "But, conscience or no conscience, I can't help thinking about her hands, and—"

"Well?"

"Why the devil do people have to eat garlic, Porfilo?"

I couldn't help breaking into a roar of laughter, and he looked at me in a hurt way.

"However," said he, "that won't keep me from going back to face the music. I told her that I loved her and that I wanted to marry her. Well, she said that she loved me and that she wanted to marry me, too. It was the infernal night and the moon, I suppose. I had chills and fevers twisting up and down inside of me, you might say. I hardly knew what I was doing. I've never felt this way about a girl before!"

"I believe that!" said I heartily.

"So I've got to go back and see her once more."

"What can you say to her?"

"I don't know! But I'll manage to find out, after a minute or two of talk, whether she's changed about me as much as I've changed about her!"

I felt that there was nothing that I could say to the point in a case like this. He was his own master, and a better master for himself, at that moment, than I could be to him. If he felt that he had to clear his mind on the subject of that girl, it was best for him to go ahead and do it. That was as far as I could carry my thinking.

So I simply said: "We've gone about eighty miles, air line from the Loveng house. We'll need two days to ride back. We'll be starting right now!"

"*We?*" said he.

"I'm going to see you through this mess," I assured him.

He pondered this for a time.

"I drag *you* back into the mess as well as myself?" he suggested.

"Not a bit! My own conscience is a pretty sleepy thing, but it's beginning to wake up a little about this. I have to go back with you. It was I that brought you to Loveng, and it was I that let him get hold of your name. Come along, Dick!"

He protested no more. We climbed into our saddles and jogged steadily along the back trail.

I think that two or three hours passed before a word was spoken, but at a time like that, one does not need words. I know that the mind of Dick Orton was filled with the same thought that was in *my* mind. What was in my mind was that I had saved a friend and gained a brother. There was a wonderful feeling of closeness. I felt as though my strength had been multiplied by twenty. In fact, I have never lost that feeling!

## · · · 11 · · ·

When we reached the house of Loveng, two days later, we paused in a screen of trees two hundred yards away. That delay was partly because we judged that it would be best to pause there until the dusk, at least, and in part because we wished to talk matters over. The chief discussion was as to whether or not we should go to the house together—as I proposed—or Dick should go alone.

The second view was the one which he maintained, and he upheld his idea with such vehemence that I had to give in to him. Because he declared that, if I would not let him go by himself, he would wait there until I changed my mind—if both of us had to starve in the meantime.

There was nothing to be done with such a state of mind in him. I kept struggling with him until after the darkness was complete, however, and even well after that. When I saw that I could do nothing whatever to change his determination, I let him. First I cautioned him to approach that house with care and to keep to cover constantly.

When he was as near to the house as cover would bring him, I advised him to wait until, by sight, or by the sound of voices, he tried to learn whether or not there was only Loveng and his family in the house, or several other men as well. In the latter case, I begged him not to continue.

After that, I had done all that I could. I let him pass on toward the house, but it was with a heavy heart that I saw him go. Loveng meant mischief. There was no doubt of that, or he would never have issued such a direct challenge to me as his statement in the paper had been.

However, I was glad to see that Dick Orton was willing to use caution in his approach to the house, no matter what might happen when the house itself was actually reached. I waited for fifteen or twenty minutes in the place where he had left me. Then I could endure it no longer, and I started out, creeping along as stealthily as I could manage it in the direction of the house and using what small cover lay before me.

I cannot tell you how peaceful and happy that scene was: The yellow flare of two lighted windows of the house of Loveng before me, and the shadowy outline of the house itself, roughened at the edges like an etching by the masses of climbing vines which tumbled over it. Even at that distance, I could smell the rank odor of the vegetable garden which the thrifty Loveng kept in cultivation on a large scale.

Or, when the wind changed a little, there was the fragrance of Mary's rose garden just ahead. Well, there was a real aroma of home about that place. Hard as I felt toward Loveng at that moment, I could not help admitting that he was the sort of stuff out of which good nations and prosperous communities are built.

It was simply that Dick Orton had touched him in the wrong place. Loveng was partly insane on the subject. He felt that he had been wronged, and that his honor demanded that he try for satisfaction. Well, it was a nasty affair to be mixed in.

My chief regard was simply for Dick, however. I had thought of Dick at first as a rather selfish, high-strung, excited, foolish boy; but I felt that he had turned into a man, and I was willing to do a great deal for him.

I pushed on toward the house until I was about sixty or seventy paces away, and directly in front of it. There I flattened myself in the wet dew behind a small shrub, and I loosened my guns in their holsters. There I waited. It seemed a long time.

To him who waits, time always drags slowly. But in the end I was glad that I had come as close as that to the house—I wished that I had come twice as far, indeed!

For, from the left—the orchard—I heard a sudden, challenging shout, followed by a sharp and rattling babel of voices, and after that a shot. Then a dozen guns, or so it seemed, roaring at once. I was on my feet, stooping low, and running as fast as my long legs could carry me over the ground.

I saw a tall form, which I had no doubt was that of Dick Orton, emerge from the shadows of the orchard and plunge across the open toward the next group of trees not thirty paces away. Behind him rushed three men—and then a fourth, all firing, but missing the dodging form of Dick until, in the very shelter of the trees, he seemed to stumble, and plunged to the ground.

I saw that part of it with the tail of my eye, so to speak. Before that I had both guns in my hands, and I was shooting hip high—or between knee and hip to be exact. There's a target almost as big as the body, and a wound there will disable almost as much as a wound through the body itself—unless the other fellow be an absolutely desperate man who fights to the last gasp.

But now I shot with both guns, and I shot at human flesh. At the very instant that Dick was falling, two of those rascals who thought nothing of taking such odds into their favor, dropped to the ground with yells that must have echoed a mile away. Certainly they were echoed from the house of Loveng by the voices of screaming women.

At the same time I shouted: "Loveng! Loveng! If you want action, look this way!"

Loveng was one of the pair I had not hit. But when he heard my voice, I saw the glint of his gun as it dropped to the ground. He threw up his hands and whirled around toward me without the slightest belly for a fight.

"Don't shoot, Meester Porfilo!" he screamed at me. "Do not shoot old man like Joe Loveng!"

There was a frightened yap out of his friend, too. His gun joined that of Joe upon the ground. At that moment, I can tell you that I blessed the storytellers who had given me a false reputation equal to twice what I was really worth. For the ridiculous name which I had been given was what won that fight for me.

Perhaps, too, it was the screaming of the tortured fellows on the ground. That was enough to unnerve most people, and besides, I had come to them from the side, and totally by surprise.

I walked up to Joe and his friend and made them

keep their arms stiff above their heads while I searched them. I took away a perfect armory from each of them, and there was no doubt at all that they had been armed for a particular purpose—the dropping of my poor Dick, who lay yonder, terribly still, and terribly silent.

I said calmly to Joe: "If Orton is alive and has a chance to recover, you have a chance, too. But if he's dead—I tell you, Loveng, that you're mortally wounded already!" I meant it, just then.

Joe Loveng and his companion wanted to look at their own wounded friends who were shrieking and begging on the ground—both of them apparently very badly hurt, though I couldn't help despising them for their noise. But I marched Joe and the other toward Dick and made them stand back to back a little distance while I examined Dick as well as I could.

He answered the first touch of my hand and voice with a groan, and then, to my exquisite satisfaction, he heaved himself to his feet.

"Dick!" I shouted at him. "Are you all right?"

"They winged me in the shoulder," he said with beautiful calm. "That knocked me on my face in this rough ground. Stunned a mite. That was all."

"Your shoulder?"

"Nothing broken," said he, as cool as you please. "I can work it a little. Painful, though, and bleeding pretty fast!"

"We'll have you in the house and tie you up in a minute," said I.

"I never want to see the inside of that house again!" said Dick in disgust.

I promised him that this would be our last visit. Then I congratulated Joe Loveng and told him that he was going to be allowed to live—as a special favor. I assure you that there was a groan of relief from Joe when he heard me speak.

In the meantime, we started back to the pair I had winged. Joe and his companion took their heads. I took a pair of knees under each arm, and though they yelled at the pain and begged us to put them down again, we carried them into the house.

Well, there was a pretty mess to look at. One big, hard-faced fellow had a bullet in his leg which had twisted around the thighbone and, entering at the hip, came down by the knee on the opposite side of the limb. When you consider that that wound was made by a .45 caliber slug, and that it was whirling as it tore through the flesh, you have an idea, faintly, of the amount of the damage that had been done to that unlucky chap.

The second of the pair was a handsome boy of about nineteen or twenty who lay grinning with pain at the ceiling and making the sign of the cross over himself from time to time as though he were trying to save his soul from devils. The slug had gone through both his legs just below the hip, and he was bleeding at a frightful rate.

As for Dick, he had a nasty cut, and no more. A bullet had glanced from the shoulder blade and across his shoulder, knocking him down. A little more off the angle, and that bullet would have driven through his heart.

He knew what he had escaped, and he was wonderfully calm about the thing. I left Loveng and his unwounded comrade to tie up the hurt legs. I gave my own attention to the shoulder of Dick, and I sang out to Mary, as she passed by with a bucket of hot water, and asked her if she wished to help.

She did not seem to hear me and went straight on to where the good-looking boy lay on the floor, making a red pool around him. There she dropped on her knees and began to work fast and hard to help her father, who would bark out at her from time to time:

"Devil of a woman! This is your work! She-devil!"

Well, in a way you have to admit that it *was* her work.

"But what does it mean?" I asked Dick. "Has she lost her hearing?"

"She has tonight," said Dick. "She met up with that bird on the floor. I'm glad you winged him! I found the pair of them on the same bench where she and *I* had sat together. But that was nine days ago, and so I suppose that she had a right to forget me.

"It peeved me, though, and I couldn't help introducing myself. That was what started trouble. Bullets began to drop like acorns, and then you jumped down out of the sky and got a little silence. Thanks, old man!"

You see by this that a big change had come over my friend, Dick Orton. He took his punishment—about the girl, which cut his pride a bit deep, I suppose; and about the wound itself—with perfect good nature.

I kept him in that house for five or six long days and nights, lying on his face, while I washed the wound and saw it began to heal after Joe Loveng, who knew something about surgery, it appeared, had sewed up the big cut. He made a good job of it too!

The wound healed with astonishing speed. The perfect quiet, and the perfect health of Dick worked in a wonderful combination. In the meantime, the other pair of wounded men recovered very slowly.

There was not much sign of improvement in either of them, but as they did not develop high temperatures, we knew at the end of that time that neither of the wounds had become infected.

In the meantime, we lived a rather odd life in that

house. They looked on the pair of us as two sticks of dynamite, at first, and I think that the entire household was convinced that, as soon as Dick was well enough to move about, I'd murder the lot of them and then leave.

However, I had only one sharp talk with my friend, Joe Loveng. I assured him that if he sent for a sheriff or a deputy, I'd kill everyone in the house before the man of the law got to me. But if I were left alone, all would be well with everyone. He swore, with a gray face, that he would treat me like an angel newly descended from heaven.

I assured him, furthermore, that while I wished him nothing but well, if he did not instantly make a trip to town and retract the statement he had made against Dick Orton, I would guarantee him a short stay on earth. He vowed that he would go in at once and tell them that he had made a mistake in the name and that it was a Dick Norton that had been with me and had assisted me to escape. Since I knew of no Dick Norton on the range, I readily decided that would do very, very well.

Joe went in, as he had promised, and had been soundly cursed by the sheriff for his first report.

After that, we got on increasingly well. Joe gradually discovered that I bore him no grudge. As for Dick, he astonished the entire household by cheerfully stating that he felt he was cheaply out of the mess. It was not very consoling for the girl, but it had a ring of truth about it that delighted Joe Loveng. From that moment he began to take care of us rather as if we had been dear friends than dreadful enemies.

There was nothing but good feeling on all sides when, at last, we left the house.

Dick's shoulder was still too bad to stand much traveling. We simply moved off into the mountains a little

distance and then we camped until he was in good
shape. Then we started for the Orton ranch and
gauged our arrival for the dark of the evening.

It was a warm night, and we found two figures sitting in rocking chairs on the Orton veranda. Somebody
in the bunkhouse was tormenting a guitar, and a cow
lately robbed of a calf, I suppose, was bawling in the
distance. But there is so much space in a Western night
that two such sounds as these could not ruin the peace
of the evening.

We rode up close to the veranda, and Dick muttered to me: "There they are together. Now, do I get
the devil?"

"Not a bit of it," I told him.

"But I deserve it," he said gloomily. "They ought to
kick me out for a tramp!"

He swung down from the saddle and began to approach.

"Hello!" sang out old man Orton. "Who's there?"

Dick made no answer, but went on a little more
quickly. At this, his father jumped up in apparent
alarm.

"Who's that?" he called sharply.

"Dick!"

What a cry from the pair of them! I reined my horse
back a bit, but still I could not help remaining
to eavesdrop on them for a moment. I saw them standing side by side. I saw them reach out their arms to
their big son as he leaped up the steps of the porch.
Then they were all tied together in one knot, and I
could hear Mrs. Orton weeping hysterically.

That was all I saw as I turned my horse and jogged
away.

Then I heard the voice of Dick shouting: "Leon!
Oh, Lee!"

I put my horse to a canter, and the noise of the hoofs drowned his voice.

I was afraid that he would be foolish enough to pursue me to bring me into that happy gathering, but he had more sense than that. No horse started after me, and I was allowed to pass over the hills unmolested and journey on into the night alone.

But not as much alone as I had been in the years before. When a man has found a friend, he cannot leave him, really, for it is my conviction that we carry something of the souls of our friends with us around the world.

Well, in a way, Dick had a heavy burden of debt to me, because that matter of the stage robbery was as yet unsolved, but I had an infinite trust in what the influence and money and honesty of old Orton would accomplish in that respect. In the meantime, with the ghosts of Father McGuire and Lawton and Mike O'Rourke, I had the new thought of Dick Orton to keep me company. I felt, as I galloped through the back of the night, that I was more to be envied than to be pitied.

## ··· 12 ···

I hadn't seen Mike for three months. You see, it was right after the Sam Dugan murder which some fools hung on me. Of course, Lawton hadn't the least idea in the world that I could have done such a rotten, treacherous thing. But they stirred up such a fuss that I didn't dare to try to slip in to see Mike. Because everyone had known for years that I loved Mike and got down to see her once in a while, and when things were pretty hot, they used to watch her house.

So when I finally went down to see her, Sheriff Lawton crossed my way with three hard-riding man-getters. Every man-jack of them was on a faster nag than my mule, but I kept Roanoke in the rough going, and Dick Lawton was foolish enough to follow right on my heels instead of throwing a fast man out on my course. For he knew what that course was, but it was a sort of unwritten law between us that if I got into the mouth of the little valley where the O'Rourke house stood, I was free.

That may sound specially generous on his side. But it wasn't—altogether. Twice he had pushed his posse up that ravine after me, and it almost cost him his next election. Because that ravine twisted like a snake, back and forth, and it was set out with shrubs and trees as thick as a garden.

I simply laid up in a comfortably shady spot, and when the boys came rushing around the bend, I let them have it. So easy that I didn't have to shoot close to a dangerous spot. I could pick my targets. However, I think that there were half a dozen bad wounds in arms and legs. Also, I pulled too far to the left on one boy and drilled him through the body. So, as I say, the sheriff nearly lost his election after that because it was said that he had ridden his men into a mantrap.

So far as Dick Lawton was concerned, I knew that that valley was forbidden as a hunting ground to him. Of course, I could trust Dick as far as he could trust me—that is to say, to the absolute limit. Because, except when we were shooting at each other, we were the best friends in the world. I know that Dick never shot extra straight at me, and I know that I never shot straight at him. My guns simply wobbled off the mark when I caught him in the sights.

Well, as I was saying, I kept old Roanoke in the rough where he could run four feet to the three of any horse that ever lived—for the simple reason that a mule's feet and skin are a lot tougher than a horse's. By the time I got across the valley, there was a clean furlong between me and Dick Lawton's boys.

So I took off my hat and said good-by to them with a wave that was nearly my last act in life. Because just as I put that hat back on my head a .32-caliber Winchester slug drilled a clean little hole through the brim a quarter of an inch from my forehead.

I've noticed that when a fellow stops to make a

grandstand play of that sort, he generally gets into pretty hot trouble. I sent Roanoke into the brush with a dig of the spurs, but the minute I was out of sight, I knew that there was no trouble left.

But I didn't slow up Roanoke. I didn't even stop to roll a cigarette, for I was eager to see Mike. I slithered up the ravine until I got a chance to squint at the ridge, and there I found a little green flag, jerking up and down and in and out in the wind, on top of the O'Rourke house. I knew that was the work of Mike's father. I think that every day of his life the old man went snooping through the woods to see if the land lay quiet. If it was, he tagged the house with that little green flag—green for Ireland, of course!—and then when someone was laying for me near the house, he would hang up a white flag.

When I saw the green I dug into Roanoke and sent that mule hopping straight to the house. As I hit the ground, I heard old man O'Rourke singing out inside the screen door of the porch: "Hey, Chet! Here's Roanoke to put up, and sling a feed of barley into him. Hey, Mother, come and look at that doggone mule! Hey, Mike, there's that Roanoke mule wanderin' around loose in the yard!"

Chet O'Rourke came first, and his old mother at his shoulder, and then the old man came next. I grabbed all their hands. It was like stepping into a shower of happiness, I tell you, to get among people where the feel of their eyes was not like so many knives pointed at you!

But I brushed through them pretty quick. I wanted Mike.

"Hey, Mike!" yelped old O'Rourke. "Ain't you comin' to see Roanoke?"

He laughed. I suppose that he was old enough to enjoy a foolish joke like that. I heard Mike sing out from the stairs beyond the front parlor. I reached the bottom of those stairs the same minute she did and caught her.

She said: "Chester O'Rourke, will you take this man away from me?"

I kicked the door shut in Chet's face and sat Mike on the window sill where the honeysuckle showered down behind her like green water, if you follow my drift. It would have done you good to stand there where I was standing and see her smile until the dimple was drilled into one cheek. She began to smooth her dress and pat her hair.

"My Lord," said I, "I'm glad to see you."

"You've unironed me," said Mike. "Just when I was all crisped up for the afternoon!"

"Have they nailed the right man for the Dugan murder?" said I. Because I was as keen about that as I was about Mike.

"They've got the right man, and he's confessed," said she.

I lowered myself into a chair and took a deep breath.

"*That's* fixed, then," said I.

"*That's* fixed," said she.

"Why do you say it that way?" said I.

"How old are you, Leon?" said she.

"I'm twenty-five."

"How old does that make me?" said Mike.

"Twenty-three."

"That's right too. How long have you been asking me to marry you?" said Mike.

"Seven years," said I.

"Well," said she, "the next time you ask me, I'm going to do it!"

"Law or no law?" said I.

"Law or no law," said she.

It made my head spin, of course, when I thought of marrying Mike and trying to make a home for her while a hundred or so cowpunchers and sheriffs and deputies, et cetera, were spending their vacation trying to grab me and the twenty thousand dollars that rested on top of my head as a reward. I moistened my lips and tried to speak. I couldn't make a sound.

"You know that I've done what I could," said I.

"I do," said she. "But now things are different."

"What do you mean?"

"William Purchass Shay is the governor, now," said she.

"What difference does that make?"

"He's a gentleman," said she.

"Well?"

"I think he'd listen to reason," said Mike.

"You want me to go to see him?"

"Just that."

"I see myself handing in my name at his office," said I. "I guess he's not too much of a gentleman to want to make twenty thousand dollars."

"Money has spoiled you, Lee," said Mike.

"Money? How come?"

"You're so used to thinking about how much you'll be worth when somebody drills a rifle ball through you —that it's turned your head."

"Are you talking serious?"

"Dead serious," said she. "Besides, you're not the only one that folks have to talk about now."

"I don't understand."

"Jeffrey Dinsmore is the other one."

Of course, I had heard about Dinsmore. He was the Texas man whose father left him about a million dollars in cattle and real estate, besides a talent for shooting straight and a habit of using that talent. Finally he killed a man where "self-defense" wouldn't work, because it was proved that Dinsmore had been layin' for him. The last heard, Dinsmore was drifting for the mountains.

"Is Dinsmore in these parts?" I asked Mike.

"He showed up in town last week and sat down in the restaurant—"

"Disguised?"

"Yes, disguised with a gun that he put on the table in front of his plate. They didn't ask any questions, but just served him as fast as they could."

"Nobody went to raise a crowd?"

"The dishwasher did, and a crowd gathered at the front door and the back."

"What happened?"

"Dinsmore finished eating and then put on his hat and walked out."

"Good Lord, what nerve! Did he bluff out the whole crowd?"

"He did."

"What's on him?"

"Just the same that's on you. Twenty thousand iron men."

"Twenty thousand dollars!" said I.

"You look sort of sad, Lee."

You'll think me a good deal of a fool, but I confess that I was staggered to find that there was another crook in the mountains worth as much to the law as I was. Between you and me, I *was* proud because I had that little fortune on my head.

"Twenty thousand!" said I.

"Dead or alive," said Mike, with a queer, strained look on her face.

"Why do you say it that way?" said I, in a whisper.

"Don't you understand?" said Mike.

Then I *did* understand, and I stood up, feeling

pretty sick. But I saw that she was right. Something had to be done.

"I start for the governor today!" said I.

Mike simply hid her face in her hands, and I didn't wait for her to break out crying.

I saw the rest of the family for an hour or so before Mike came in to us. She was as clear-eyed as ever, when she came, but there was something in her face which was a spur to me. I did not wait for the night. I judged that no pursuers would be lingering for me in the valley at this late day, so I slipped out of the house finding Roanoke refreshed by his rest and a feed of grain. I went away without leaving any farewells behind me.

I cut across country, straight over the ridge of the eastern mountains. Just below timberline I camped that night—a cold, wet night—and I rode on gloomily the next morning until I was over the crest of the ridge and had a good view of the land that lay beneath me.

It was a great, smooth-sweeping valley, most of it, the ground rolling now and then into little hills—but with hardly the shadow of a tree—and so on and on to piles of blue mountains which leaned against the farther horizon. They were a good hundred miles away. Between me and that range lay the city that I had to reach.

You will agree with me that it was not a very pleasant undertaking. I had to get myself over seventy miles of open country to the capital of the State. Then I had to get seventy miles back into the mountains once more.

However, there was nothing else for it. That day I went down to the edge of the trees and the foothills, and there I rested until the verge of dusk. When that time came, I sent Roanoke out into the open and headed straight away toward the big town. He could have made the distance before daylight, but there was no point in that.

I sent Roanoke over sixty-five miles that night, however, and he was a tired mule when I dropped off his back on the lee side of a haystack. I could see the lights of the town five miles off. Not a big place, you will think, but there were thirty-five thousand people there, and that made it just about five times as large as any city I had ever seen in my life. It was simply a metropolis to me!

The dawn was only a moment away. So I walked away from the stack to a wreck of a shack in a hollow. There I turned in and slept solidly until afternoon.

I was thirsty and tired and hungry when I wakened. Besides that, I had a jumpy heart, and the strain of the work ahead of me was telling pretty fast! The worst part of the trip was wasting that afternoon and waiting for the night. But as a matter of fact, I didn't wait for the night.

The edge of the sun was barely down before I was streaking across open country, and there was still plenty of daylight when I cut down a bridle path near the edge of the town and met an old fellow coming up. He was riding bareback, and I shall never forget how his white beard was parted by the wind.

He gave me a very cheerful "howd'ye," and I waved back to him.

"Well, stranger," said that old man, "where are you aimin' for, if I might ask?"

"Work," said I.

"Come right along with me."

"What kind?"

He had one tooth in the right-hand corner of his upper gum. He fixed this in a wedge of chewing tobacco and worked a long time at it until he got it loose. All the while he was looking me over with popping, pale-blue eyes. I never before had noticed how close an old man can be to a child.

"Well, partner," said he, "young fellers is picky and choosy; I used to be that way myself. But when I come to get a little age behind me, why, then I seen that it didn't make so much difference what a man done. All kinds of work that ever I see gives you the same sort of an ache in the shoulders and an ache in the calves of your legs and in your brain. Ain't you noticed that?"

I told him that I had.

He said: "Same way about chuck. I used to be mighty finicky about grub. It don't make no difference to me now. Once a mite of grub is swallowed, what difference whether it was a mouthful of dry bread or a mouthful of ice cream? Can you tell me that?"

I could see that he had branched out on his special kind of information. Most old men are that way. They've got a couple of sets of ideas oiled up in their old noodles and whenever they get a chance, they'll blaze away on them. If they're interested in oil wells, you can start talking about lace and they'll get over to oil wells just as easy as if you started with derricks. I saw that this was one of that brand. However, if he would talk, I saw that he might be of some sort of use to me.

So I said: "I've been back country for a long time. I want to have a try working in town!"

He shook his head, very sad at that.

"Son," said he, "I live only two mile out, but I been to town only once this summer. That time I come home with my feet all blistered up and my head aching from the glare of the pavements. I give the town up. If I was you, I'd give it up, too."

I said nothing, but I couldn't help smiling. The old

chap began to nod and smile, too. He was a fine fellow, no doubt of that.

"Well," said he, "you can't expect folks to learn by their elders. If they did, people'd get wiser and wiser, instead of the other way. What you want to do in town?"

"Drive an ice wagon, maybe. I don't care. I never seen the town before."

"You don't say!"

"I guess that's the capitol?"

"Yes, sir. There she be. That white dome. I guess you seen it in your schoolbooks when you was a kid? There she be. Look here, ain't you been raised right around near here?"

He had sagged a little closer to me while we were looking at the town, and now I caught him batting his bleary old eyes at me behind his glasses. I knew there was danger ahead.

"No," said I. "I've never been in the big town before."

"Oh, it ain't so big. Me, I've been far as St. Louis. Now, there's a real city for you. It lays over this a mighty lot!"

"I suppose it does. But it hasn't many things finer than the capitol building, I guess!"

"Well, I dunno. It's got a lot of banks and things pretty grand with white stone posts around them. It makes a heap of noise, too. You can hear it for miles. But you can't hear nothin' here."

"Well," said I, "I suppose there are fine big houses there. The governor's house must be mighty fine!"

"Him? No, sir. William P. Shay ain't the man to live big and grand. He's livin' in his ma's old house out on Hooker Avenue—which has got so fashionable, lately, what with the park right opposite with the benches to set on. I passed that way once, and I never forget the smell of the lilacs passin' by Mrs. Shay's house! It was sure a sweet thing."

"I suppose that they're still there?"

"Yes, sir."

"Other folks got 'em, too?"

"Nary a one. Young feller, I can't get out of my head that I've seen you sure, somewheres, sometime!"

I knew very well where he'd seen me. It was in some roadside bulletin board or perhaps just a handbill nailed against a post, showing my face with big letters under it. I knew very well where he had seen me. I decided I had better start along; so I told him that I would go right on into town and get lodgings before it was too dark.

But after I had gone a little way, I leaned down as if to fix a stirrup leather and I had a chance to glance back. Old white beard was already over the hill.

I didn't suspect that he had seen too much of me. But when a man has been a fugitive from the law with a price on his head for seven years, it makes him overlook no bets. I recalled, too, that I was riding a mule, and that in itself was enough to make any man suspicious.

So I snapped back to the top of the hill and through the hollow beneath I could see the old man scooting along. He looked back over his shoulder, just then, and when he saw me, he doubled up like a jockey putting up a fast finish down the stretch and began to burn his whip into that old horse he was riding.

I shouldn't have done it, of course. But I couldn't help wanting to make his fun worthwhile. So I fired a shot straight into the air.

I heard his yell come quavering back to me; and after that the horse seemed to take as much interest in the running as his rider did. He hunched himself like a loafer wolf trying to shove himself between his front legs while he beats for cover.

It was a mighty funny thing to watch. I laughed till I was crying. By that time the old man had disappeared in the night and the distance. Then I turned around and saw that I had a big job to do and to do fast, because as soon as that old fogy got to a house with a telephone in it, he would plaster the news all over town that Leon Porfilo, on his mule, was heading straight for them, ready to make trouble, and lots of it!

How many scores of men and boys would clean up their old guns and start hunting for me, I could only guess.

But right there I made up my mind that I couldn't enter that town on a mule. I put old Roanoke away in a little hollow where there were trees enough to shelter him and a brook in the center to give him water and plenty of long, coarse grass among the trees for provender.

Then I shoved my guns into my clothes and started hiking for the town. It was mighty risky, of course, because if trouble started I was a goner. But I decided that I'd be a lot less looked for on foot. You'll wonder, perhaps, why I didn't wait a few days under cover before I went in. But I knew that the next morning a hundred search parties would be out for me, unless I was already in jail.

## ··· 13 ···

It was not so bad as I had expected. A city of that size, I thought, would be so filled with people that my only good refuge would be in the very density of the crowd, but when I reached the outskirts, I found only unpaved streets and hardly anyone on the sidewalks saving the few workingmen who were hurrying home late to their suppers. And what a jumble of suppers! One acquires an acute nose in the mountains or on the desert, and I picked out at least fifty different articles of cookery before I had covered the first block.

I started on the second with a confused impression of onions, garlic, frying steak, stew, boiled tomatoes, cabbage, bacon, coffee, tea, and too many other things to mention. Nasally speaking, that first block of the capital town was like the first crash of a symphony orchestra. I went on very much more at ease through block after block with almost no one in sight, until I came to broad paved streets where there was less dust flying in the air—and where the front yards were not simply hard-beaten dirt with a plant or two at the corners of the houses.

For here there were houses set farther back. Some had hedges at the sidewalk—but all had gardens, and most of the way one could look over blocks and blocks of neatly cropped lawns, with flower borders near the houses, and flowering shrubs set out on the lawns. There were scores and scores of watering spouts whirling the spray into the air with a soft, delightful whispering.

They all had a different note. Some of them rattled around slowly and methodically like so many dray wheels, throwing out a spray in which you could distinguish each ray of water all the way round. There were some singing and spinning and making a solid flash like the wheel of a bright-painted buggy when a horse is doing a mile in better than three minutes.

Once in a while a breeze dipped out of the sky and stirred the heavy, hot air of the street, and blew little mists of the sprinklers to me and gave me quick scents of flowers. But always there was that wonderful odor of the ground drinking, and drinking.

I felt very happy, I'll tell you. I felt very expansive and kindly to the whole human race. Now and then I'd see a man run down the steps of his house and go out in his shirt sleeves, and take hold of the hose, and curse softly when the spray hit him, and then give the sprinkler a jerk that moved the little machine to another place. Like as not, he jerked the sprinkler straight toward him.

Then he would duck for the sidewalk and stand there wiping his face and hands with a handkerchief and stamping the water from his shoes and "phewing" and "damning" to himself as though he were ashamed.

But before they went back into the house, each

man would stop a minute, and look at the grass and
the shrubs, each beaded with water and pearled with
the light of the nearest street lamps—and then up to
the trees—and then up to the stars—and then go
slowly into the house, singing, most like, and stepping
light. When those men lifted their heads and looked
up into the sky like that, I knew that they saw
heaven.

When one young fellow ran out from his front
door, I saw a girl come to the window and look after
him, and hurry him with: "The soup will be stone
cold, Archie."

I couldn't help it. I stopped short and leaned a
hand against a tree and watched him move the sprinkler. Then, humming under his breath, he ran for the
house. There were springs under that boy's toes, I tell
you. From what I could see of the girl, I didn't wonder. But at his front door he turned and saw me still
standing under the tree, watching and aching and
groaning to myself:

"Mike and me—when do we get our chance—
when do we get our chance!"

He called out: "Hey, you—what you want?"

A mighty snappy voice—like the home dog growling at a stranger pup. He was being defensive.

"Nothing," said I.

"Then hump yourself—move along!" said he.

Perhaps you'll think that I might have been angered by that. But I wasn't. I was only pretty well
sickened and saddened. If ever I were caught—and
this night there was a grand chance that the law
would take me—the dozen men in the jury box would
be no better than this fellow—a clean-living fellow,
with his heart in the right place—but snarling when
he saw a strange dog near his house! Human nature—
I knew it—and I didn't blame him.

"All right. I'll move along," said I.

I only shifted one tree down and stopped again. You see, I wanted to watch that fellow go striding into his house and into that dining room and watch his wife smile at him.

Sentimental bunk? I know that as well as you do, but when a man has lived alone for seven years with mountains, and above timberline most of the time—seven winters, you know—well, it makes him either a murderer or a softy. I hardly know which is worse! But I was not a murderer, no matter what the world might say of me.

The householder had a glimpse of me again as he swung open his front door, and he came flaring back at me with the running stride of an athlete. I saw that he was big, and big in the right places.

He was in front of me in another moment.

"I'm going!" said I, and I turned and started shambling away.

He caught me by the shoulder and whirled me around.

"Look here!" said he. "I don't like the looks of you—and the way you hang around—who are you?"

I shrank back from him against a tree. "A poor bum, mister," said I. "I don't want no trouble. But I was lookin' through the window. It looked sort of homelike in there."

"You're lying!" said he. "By heaven, I'll wager you're some second-story crook. I've a mind—"

He put his hand on me again.

You'll admit that I'd taken a good deal from him. But it's easy for a big man to take things from other people. I don't know why that is. Little fellows always have a chip on their shoulders.

But big fellows learn when they're young that they're not to fight—because they're always too big for the other boys! But still, I was a bit angry when this young husband began to force his case at my expense. There were two hundred and twenty pounds of me, but down to the very last pound of me, I was hot.

Just then the girl's voice sang out: "Archie! Archie! What are you doing—oh!"

There was a little squeal at the end as she sighted me.

"You see?" said I. "Let me go. I won't trouble you any. You're scaring your wife to death, you fool!"

"What? You impudent rat—"

He started a first-rate punch from the hip, but I caught his wrist and doubled his arm around behind him in a way which must have been new to him. He was a strong chap. But he hadn't my incentive, and he hadn't my training.

We stood with our faces inches apart. Suddenly he wilted.

"Porfilo!" said he through his teeth.

"Do you think I'm going to sink a slug in you?" I asked.

I saw by the look of his eyes that he did, and it made me a pretty sick man, I can tell you! I dropped his arm, and I went off down that street not caring a great deal whether I lived or died.

I went down that street until it carried me bang up against the capitol building in the middle of the great big square. Off to the right was the beginning of the park. I went off down the street that faced on it.

I think I must have passed five hundred people in that square, but I'm certain that not one of them guessed me. It would have been too queer to find Leon Porfilo *walking* through a street. They passed me by one after another—which shows that we see only what we expect to see.

In the street opposite the park it was easy going

again. It was a fairly dark street, because there were
no lamps except at the corner, and the blocks were
long. Lamps on only one side of the street, too—because the park was on the other side and that was a
thrifty town!

I walked about half a mile, I suppose, from the
central square and then I found the house without
looking for it. It was simply a great outwelling fragrance of the lilacs, just as the old man had told me.
There was the yard filled with big shrubs—almost
trees of 'em, and in the pool of darkness around the
trees were rows and spottings of milk-white lilies.

It was a good thing to see, that yard. It was so filled
with beauty—I don't know exactly how to say it. It
was filled with hominess, too. I felt as though I had
opened that squeaking gate a hundred times before
and stepped down onto the brick path where the grass
that grew between the bricks crunched under my
heels.

Then I sidestepped from the path and among the
trees. I went to the side of the house. I climbed up to
the window in time to see the ceremony begin. About
a dozen people piled into the room—and when the
seating was over, a grim-faced, middle-aged man sat
at the head of the table and a pretty-faced girl of
twenty-one or so at the other.

Then I remembered that the governor's wife was
not half his age.

I thought I understood one reason for the tired look
in his face! In the meantime, there was nothing for
me to do for a time. So I found a bench among the
trees and lay down on it to watch the stars.

I waited until the smell of food went through me,
and I tugged up my belt two notches. I waited until
the humming voices and the laughter that always begin a meal—even a mountain dinner—died off into a

broken talking—noise of dishes. Then music, somewhere. Well, I was never educated up to appreciating
the squeaking of a violin!

A long time after that, somebody was making a
speech. I could hear the steady voice. I could almost
hear the yawns.

Somehow, I pitied the pretty girl at the far end of
the table!

## ··· 14 ···

I waited a full hour after that. Then people began to leave the house, and finally, when the front door opened and closed no more, I began my rounds of the house. I found what I wanted soon enough. It was not in the second story, but a lighted window in the first, and I had a step up, only, to get a view of the inside of the room, and a broad-gauge window sill to hang to while I watched.

The window was open, which made everything easier. There was not much chance for me to be betrayed by the noise I might make in stirring about, for the wind was dipping and rustling among the trees.

I was looking into a high, narrow room with walls covered with books, and queer, old-looking framed photographs above the bookcases. There was a desk that looked as solid as rock. In front of the desk was the governor. I could have told that it was the governor even if I'd never seen him before, because he had that gone look about the eyes and those wrinkles of too much smiling that come to men who have offices of state. A man like that, when his face is at rest, is simply giving up thanks that he's not offending anyone.

The governor had a man sitting beside his desk—a man who looked only less tired than the governor himself. He was scribbling shorthand while the governor turned over and fiddled at a pile of papers on his desk and kept talking softly and steadily. All sorts of letters.

Well, he had to dictate so many letters, and make them all so different, that I wondered what fellow's brain could be big enough to hold so much stuff, and so many different kinds. I suppose that in that hour he dictated more letters than I'd ever written in my life. I could see new reasons every minute for that tired look. I began to think that he must know everyone in the State.

I heard the secretary ask him if he needed him any longer. I saw the governor look up quickly at him and then stand up and clap him on the shoulder and say:

"Go home to sleep! I've not been paying enough attention to you, but forgive me!"

I saw the secretary fairly stagger out of the room. Then there was the governor sitting over the typewriter and reading his correspondence on the one hand and picking at the machine with one finger on the other, and swearing in between in a style that would have tickled the ears of any cowpuncher on the hardiest bit of the range.

I didn't hear anyone tap at the door. But pretty soon he jumped up with the look of a man about to accept ten million dollars. He opened the door and the pretty, young wife stood there wrapped up to the chin in a dressing gown. She looked him up and down in a way that smeared the smile off his face and left a sick look that I had seen there before.

It was an old-fashioned house, and there was a transom over the door. She pointed at the open transom and said half a dozen words out of stiff lips. She didn't say much. Just enough. A bullet isn't very big, either, but if it's planted in the right place it will tear the heart out of a man.

She jerked about on her heel and flounced away, and the governor leaned against the wall for a minute with all the sap run out of him. Then he closed the door and the transom and went back to the typewriter.

He was pretty badly jarred, though, and he sat there for a moment all loose, like a fellow with the strength run out of him. Then he shook his head and set his jaw and began to batter that typewriter again. I could see that he was a game sort of a man. Mighty game and proud and clean; I liked him all the way through; and yet I felt a mite sorry for the girl wife, too, when I thought of the way the governor's language must have been sliding out through that transom and percolating through the house. I suppose that a real respectable house would take a couple of generations to work language like that out of the grain of it!

I slid a leg inside the window, and made just enough noise for the governor to stop work and sit with his head up; and his right hand went back to his hip pocket—and came away again.

I stepped inside the room and was standing there pretty easy when he turned around.

He didn't jump up or start yapping for help or doing anything else that was foolish. He just sat and looked me over.

"Well, Porfilo," said he at last, "I suppose that you've tried to work out the most popular spectacular job in the State and decided that the governor's house was the best place for it. Is that it?"

I merely grinned. I knew that he would take it something like that, but it was mighty good to hear him talk up. It sent a tingle through all the right places in me. I just took off my hat and made myself easy.

"What do you want?" said he, frowning as I smiled. "My wallet?"

He tossed it to me. I caught it and threw it back. I had both my hands. Somehow, I hated to show a gun to that man.

"Something bigger than that?" said he, sneering. "I suppose that you'll want the papers to know how you held up the governor without even showing a gun?"

I got hot at that; in the face, I mean.

"No, sir," said I. "I'm not a rat."

"Tell me what you want," said he through his teeth. "There was a time when I served as a sheriff in this State, young man. There was a time when I carried guns. Now the fewer moments I spend with you, the better."

"Governor," said I, "do you think I'm a plain skunk?"

"No," said he, very brisk, and with his eyes snapping. "I should call you whatever you please—a purple, spotted, striped, or garden variety of skunk. Never the common sort! Now what do you want with me, young man, if you don't want money? Is it a pardon?"

There was so much honest scorn in the governor's face, to say nothing of his voice, that all the starch went out of me. I could only mumble, "Yes, sir, that's what I want."

He threw up both his hands—such a quick gesture that it made a gun jump out of my pocket as quick as a snake's head out of a hole. I couldn't help it! But he saw the movement and he sneered again.

"Porfilo," said he, "I suppose you are going to threaten to shoot me unless I turn over a signed pardon to you?"

I shoved that gun away in my clothes. I was beginning to get angry in turn.

"I've come to talk, not to shoot," said I. "I've come to play your own dirty game with you!"

"Is my game dirty?" said he through his teeth.

Oh, yes, he was a fighting man, that governor! I wished that his young wife could have seen him then.

"Isn't it," said I, "a lot dirtier than mine? You beg people for their votes."

"Entirely false," said he. "But I enjoy a moral lecture from a murderer."

"I never murdered a man in my life," said I.

It made him blink a little.

"But you," said I, and I jabbed a finger into the air at him, "you get up and talk pretty sweet to a lot of swine that you hate."

He parted his lips to answer me, but then he changed his mind and sat back in his chair and watched me.

"About the murders," I went on. "I never shot a man unless he tackled me to kill me."

He parted his lips again to speak, but again he changed his mind and smiled.

"You are an extraordinarily simple liar," said he.

It's a good deal to be called a liar and swallow it. I didn't swallow this very well.

I snapped back at him: "Governor, I came here to see you because I was told that you're a gentleman."

"Well, well, Porfilo," said he, a little red. "Who told you that?"

"A girl," said I.

*The* girl?" said he.

"Yes," said I.

"Good heavens, Porfilo," said he, "are you going to try to hide behind a woman who loves you?"

"I don't hide," said I. "What I ask you to do, is to go down the record against me and figure out where I've sunk lead into anybody that wasn't gunning for me. Was there ever a man I sank that wasn't a gun fighter and a crook before he ever started after me? There never was!

"I've ridden a hundred miles to get out of the way of trouble, when trouble was showing up in the shape of a clean, decent man. But when a thug came after me, I didn't budge. Why should I?"

"Well," said he, "I'll tell you what you've done. You've made me listen to you. But just the other day Sheriff Lawton had two fine citizens shot by you."

"Leg and arm," said I.

"Yes, they were lucky."

"Lucky?" said I. "Do you think it was lucky, governor? If I've practiced hard at shooting every day of my life for the last ten years, at least, do you think that I'm so bad that I miss at forty yards? No, governor, you don't think that. Nor do you think that I've stood up to so few men that I get buck fever when I have a sight of 'em. No, sir, you don't think that, either!"

The governor scratched his chin and blinked at me. But I was pretty pleased, because I could see that he was getting more reasonable every minute.

"I don't mind admitting," said he, "that I'm inclined to believe the nonsense that you're talking." He grinned very frankly at me. However, I saw that I still had a long way to go.

"Are you armed?" said I.

"No," said he, "because very often in my official life I have a desire to use a gun. And I'm past the age when pleasures like that are becoming."

"Are you taking me serious?" said I.

"More than any judge would," said he.

"I believe you!" said I, and I couldn't help a quaver in my voice.

I saw that that put back my cause several lengths and would make the rest of the running pretty hard for me.

He said in that stiff way of his: "Have no sentimental nonsense, Porfilo!"

"I'm sorry," said I. Then I burst out with the truth at him, because I could see that there was no use trying to bamboozle him.

"A man can't help feeling sorry for himself when he gets a chance," said I.

The governor twisted up his mouth, and then he laughed. It did me a lot of good to hear him laugh, just then.

"As a matter of fact," said he, "not so long ago I was pitying myself! Now, young man, I think I can say that I like you. But that won't keep me for an instant from trying to have you hanged by the neck until you're dead."

"Do you mean that?" said I.

"I'm too tired to talk foolishness that I don't mean," said he. "I'll tell you what, Porfilo. If a petition for your pardon were signed by a thousand of the finest citizens in this State, that petition would have no more chance than a snowball in hell!"

He meant it, well enough, and I could see that he did. It made me within a shade of as sick as I'd ever been in my life.

"Well?" said he.

"I'm studying," said I, "because I know that I've got something more to say, but I can't figure out what it is!"

The governor laughed. He said: "I come closer to liking you every minute. But why is it that you think that you have something more to say?"

"Because," said I, "I know that I'm an honest man and a peaceable man!"

He laughed again, and I didn't like his laughter so well, this time.

"Well," said he, "I won't interrupt you!"

"You *know* that I'm a crook?" I asked him.

"About as well as any man could know anything."

"Have you looked up my whole life?"

"A few chunks of it have been served up to me— such as the Sam Dugan murder."

"The rest of your information is about as sound as that!" I snapped back at him, thanking heaven for the chance. "The murderer of Dugan has confessed and is in jail now!"

The governor blinked at me. "I didn't know that," muttered he.

"Of course you didn't," I cried to him. "Every time they have a chance to hang a crime on the corner of my head, that makes first-page news. Every time they don't know who fired the shot that killed, they say: 'Porfilo!' But when they find out the facts a couple of days later, it makes poor reading. So they stick the notice back among the advertisements—"

The governor nodded. I could see him accepting my idea and confessing that there was something in it.

"Well," said I, "I ask you to start in and look up my life. It won't be hard to do. One of your secretaries can unload the whole yarn for you in about half a day's work. Then sift out the proved things from the unproved. Give me the benefit of a doubt!"

"That sort of benefit will never win you a pardon from me," said he.

"I don't want a charity pardon," said I.

"What kind do you expect?"

"An earned one!"

"Confound it," said the governor, rubbing his hands together, "I like your style. Now tell me how under heaven you are going to win a pardon from *me*."

"You've heard of Jeffrey Dinsmore," said I.

"I have," said he.

"Is he as bad as I am—according to reputation?"

"Dinsmore is a—" he began. Then he shut his teeth carefully, and breathed a couple of times. "I should say that he's as bad as you are," said he between his teeth.

"All right," said I. "Here's my grand idea that brought me as close to the rope as the capital city, here!"

"Blaze away," said he.

"Dinsmore has twenty thousand dollars on his head, same as me."

"I understand that."

"We're an even bet, then?"

"I suppose so, if you want to make a sporting thing out of it."

"All right," said I. "What's better than two bad men—"

"One, I suppose," said the governor. "But I wish you wouldn't be so darned Socratic."

I didn't quite understand what he meant, so I drilled away.

"The catching of me has been a pretty hard job," said I. "It's cost the State seven years—and they haven't got me yet. But it's cost them a lot for the amount of money that they've spent hunting me."

"Besides your living expenses," said the governor with a twisted grin that hadn't much fun in it.

I caught him up on that.

"My living expenses have come out of the pockets of other crooks. I've never taken a penny from an honest man. Look up my record!" said I.

At this, he seemed really interested, and sat up and rubbed his fine square chin and scowled at me—not in anger, but as if he were trying to search my character.

"Well," said he, "you are the darndest crook I've ever heard of—with twenty thousand on your head and pretending to live like an honest man!"

"For seven years!" I said, rubbing the facts in on him.

"Aye," said he, "but will you insist that you've been honest all the time?"

"I helped in one robbery, and then I returned the money to the bank. You can get the facts on that, pretty easy. I had about a quarter of a million in my hands."

"If you have a record like that, why hasn't something been done for you?"

"I was waiting," said I, "for a governor that was a gentleman; and here I am."

"Ah, well," said he, "of course I'll have to look into this. It can't be right. Yet I can't help believing you. But what is this about earning your pardon?"

"I was saying that the State had spent a good many tens of thousands on me, and there doesn't seem to be much chance of it letting up on the expenses right away!"

He nodded.

"This Jeffrey Dinsmore is a fellow with lots of friends and with a family with money behind him. It will surely cost a lot to get at him!"

"It will!" said the governor with a blacker face than ever.

"I want to show you the shortest way out."

"I'm ready to listen, now. What's in your head, young man?"

"Let Dinsmore know the proposition. I say, let it be a secret agreement between you and me—and Dinsmore—that if he brings me in—dead or alive—you'll see that he gets a pardon, and the reverse goes for me."

The governor stared at me with his eyes enlarged. He began by shaking his head.

I cut in very softly—hardly loud enough to interrupt his thoughts.

"I can promise you that there'll be no living man brought in. One of us will have to die. There's no doubt about that!"

"I know that," said William Purchass Shay. "I believe you, Porfilo. By the way, are you Mexican?"

"My mother was Irish," said I. "Away back yonder, there was a dash of Mexican Indian in my father's blood."

It seemed to me that his smile was a lot easier when he heard that! Then he got up and took my hand.

"After all," he said, "one gets good laws in operation by hard common sense." He paused. "Is there anything that you need, Porfilo?"

"Wings to get out of this town!" said I.

He nodded very gravely. "I don't see how the devil you got into it."

"Walked," said I.

"While they were looking for a man on a mule! That was the alarm that came in—from the old man you shot at! Did you shoot at him, Porfilo?"

"The old scamp was burning up the country to get to a telephone and blow the news about me. So I thought I'd give him a real thrill and I fired into the air. That's all there was to it!"

"There's seventy miles between you and the mountains where you are so safe," said he.

"Open country!" I nodded. "Seventy miles to Mr. Dinsmore, too!"

"Are you sure of that?" asked the governor, with a start.

"Why, that's where the report located him."

"The report lied, then! It lied like the devil!"

He said it in such a way that I could not answer him. I held my tongue until he reached out a sudden hand and wrung mine, and his eyes were fixed on the floor.

"Good luck to you—the best of luck to you, Porfilo!" said he.

I slid through the window, and when I looked back, I saw him standing just as I had left him, with his eyes fixed upon the floor.

Well, I couldn't make it out at the time, but I figured pretty close, and I was reasonably sure that something I had brought into his mind connected with the idea of his wife, and that was what had taken the starch out of him.

However, I was not thinking about the governor ten seconds later. For, as I dropped from the window for the ground beneath, I saw a glint like that of a star through thin clouds. But this glimmer was among the leaves of some shrubbery, and I knew that it was a touch of starlight on the polished barrel of a gun!

## ··· 15 ···

Well, when you hear people speak of lightning thinking, I suppose that you smile and call it "talk"—but
between the time I saw that glimmer of a gun in the
brush and the instant my heels hit the ground beneath,
I can give you my word that I had figured everything
out.

If I were caught, people would want to know what
Leon Porfilo had been doing in the governor's office.
Even if I were not caught, it would be bad enough.
Because there would be no end of chatter all over the
State. But, as a matter of fact, if I wanted to help the
reputation of a man who had given me a mighty
square deal, the best way for it was to cut out of
those premises without using a gun or even drawing
one.

I say that I thought of these things while I was
dropping from the window to the ground, and I hadn't
much time besides that, for as I hit the ground and

flopped over on my hands to ease the shock, I saw a big fellow with two more behind him step out of the brush and the lilacs about five paces away. Five paces —fifteen feet!

Well, you look across the room you are in and it seems quite a distance, at that. Besides, I had the night in my favor. But I give you my word that when I looked at those three silhouettes cut out against the starlit lilac bloom behind them, and when I saw the big pair of gats in the hands of the leader—and the gun apiece in the hands of the men behind—well, I knew in the first place that if I tried to run either side, they'd have me against the white background of the house and fill me with lead before I had taken two steps. I turned that idea over in the fifth part of a second while the leader was growling in a professionally ugly way—if you've ever heard a detective make an arrest, you'll know what I mean.

"You—straighten up and tuck your hands over your head pronto!"

"All right!" muttered I.

He could not have distinguished the first part of my movement from an honest surrender. For I simply began to straighten as he had told me to do. The difference was in my right hand—a five-pound stone. As my hands flew up, that stone jumped straight into the stomach of the leader.

Both his guns went off, and there was a silvery clashing of broken window glass behind me. One of those bullets was in a big scrub oak. The other had broken the window of the governor's office and broken the nose of the photograph of Shay's grand-dad—and drilled through the wall itself.

But the holder of the two guns threw out his hands to keep from falling, and in doing that he backhanded his two assistants. One of them started shooting blindly. The other dropped his gun, but he had enough sand and wit to make a dive for me. I clubbed him over the head with my fist, as though it were a hammer, and very much as though a hammer had struck him, he curled up. I almost tripped over him. By the time I had disentangled my feet, the chief was shooting from the ground.

But he was a long distance from doing me any real harm. The nerves of those three were a good deal upset. I suppose, in fact, that they had not had much experience in trying to arrest men who can't afford to go behind the bars and be tried for their lives.

At any rate, I was lost among those lilacs in a twinkling. At the same time, a considerable ruckus broke out in the house. Windows began to be thrown up, and voices were shouting, and the three detectives themselves were making enough noise to satisfy fifty.

Under cover of that racket, I didn't bolt out onto the street in the direction for which I was headed. Instead, I whirled around and under the shelter of those God-blessed lilacs, I tore back down the length of the yard.

I cleared the house—and still all the noise was in the rear and out toward the street. When I got into the back yard, I saw one discouraging thing—a tall fence about nine feet high and a man just in the act of climbing over. He had jumped up on a box; and the box had crumpled to nothing under him as he leaped. However, he had made the top of the fence.

I had to make the same height, without a box to jump from.

In the meantime, who was the man who was trying to make his getaway even before me?

I didn't stop to ask. I went at that fence with a flying leap and got my hands fixed on the top of it. With the same movement, I let my body swing like a pendulum. So I shot myself over the top a good deal like a pole vaulter.

When I let go with my hands, and while I was pendent in the air, falling, I saw that the man who had gone over ahead had stumbled just beneath me, and, like a snarling dog, he was growling at me. He fired while I was still hanging in the air, and the bullet clipped my upper lip and let me taste my own blood.

It's very bad to let an Irishman taste his own blood. It's bad enough to let one who's half Irish do the thing. At any rate, I went half mad with anger. Then I landed on him.

He wasn't big, and my weight seemed to flatten him out.

It was an alley cutting through behind the grounds of the governor's house, and there was a dull street lamp in a corner of the alley. It shed not very much light, but enough to show me a handsome-faced young fellow—not made big, but delicately like a watch, you know. A sensitive face, I called it.

He was too small for hitting. I just picked him up while he was winded, and then I dropped him on the pavement, which I thought might be pretty bad for that pretty face of his.

Then I started on. One thing I was glad of, and that was that there was a neat-looking horse tethered at the end of the alley, and from the length of the stirrups—as I made the saddle in a flying leap—I sort of thought that it might have belonged to the fellow I had just left behind me.

I cut the tethering rope from the saddle with my sheath knife, and then I scooted that horse across the street and down another alley.

I pulled him up walking into the next street beyond and jogged along as though nothing particularly concerning me were happening that night. A very good way to get through with trouble. But the trouble was that there was still hell popping at the governor's house. I could hear their voices—and more than that, I could hear their guns, and so could half of the rest of the town.

People were piling out of every house, and more than one man who was legging in the danger direction yelped at me as I went past and asked where I was going. But that was not so bad. I didn't mind questions. What I wanted to avoid was personal contact!

Here half a dozen fellows on fine horses took the corner ahead of me on one wheel, so to speak, spilling out all across the street as they raced the turn. When they saw me, one of them shouted: "What are you riding *that* way for?"

I knew that they would be halfway down the block before they could stop, and besides, I hoped that they wouldn't be too curious if I didn't answer.

So I just trotted the horse around the same corner by which they had come. But one question unanswered wasn't enough for them. They were like hungry dogs, ready to follow any trail.

"Hello?" yelled the sharp, biting voice of that same leader, to whom I began to wish bad luck. "No answer from that gent. Let's have a look at his face!"

I could hear the scraping and the scratching of the hoofs of the horses as the riders turned them in the middle of the block with cowpuncher yells that took down my temperature at least a dozen degrees.

In the meantime, I was not marking time. I scooted my mount down the next block. The minute he took his first stride I knew that the race would be a hot one, no matter how well they were fixed with horses. Because that little horse was a wonder! I never put eyes on him after that night, but he ran with me like a jack rabbit—a long-winded jack rabbit, at that!

My weight was such a puzzler for him, that he grunted with every stride, but he whipped me down that street so fast that I had nearly turned west on the next corner before the pursuit sighted me. But I failed by the stretched-out tail of that little Trojan; and by the yell behind me I knew that they were riding hard and riding for blood.

I turned again at the next corner, and as I turned, I saw that two men were riding even with me. They had even gained half a length in the running of that block!

I made up my mind right away. If they had speed, they could show it in a straightway run, because it kills a little horse to dodge corners with a heavy man on his back. So I put my pony straight west up that street, running him on the gutter of the street where dust and leaves had gathered and made easier padding for his hoofbeats.

In a mile we were out of the town, but those six scoundrels were still hanging on my rear, and raising the country with their yells and their whoops.

I could hear others falling in behind me. There were twenty now, shoving their horses along my path. Every moment they were increasing in numbers. Besides, after the first half mile, my weight began to kill that game little horse. He ran just as fast, nearly, as he had before. But the spring was going out of his gallop. Then I was saying to him—just hold out over the hill and into the hollow—just over the hill and into the hollow.

Well, they were snapshooting at me as I went up that hill, and the hill and my weight together slowed my little horse frightfully. However, he got to the top of it at last, and my whistle was a blast between my

fingers. Fifty yards of running down that hillside—
with my poor little horse staggering and almost dying
under me. My heart stood in my mouth, for if Roanoke were gone, I was a lost man with a halter
around my neck.

But no—there he was, sloping out of the brush and
heading full tilt toward me. As I came closer, he
wheeled around and began to shamble away at his
wonderful trot in the same direction I was riding. So
I made a flying jump from the saddle of the little
horse and onto the rocklike strength of the back of
Roanoke.

## ··· 16 ···

There was not a great deal to the race after that. I suppose that there were a half a dozen horses in the lot that could have nabbed Roanoke in an early sprint. But the little gamester I rode out of town had taken the sap out of the running legs of the entire outfit.

When I left him for Roanoke, that old mule carried me up the course of the hollow—where water must have stood half the year, by the tree growth—and after he had run full speed for a few minutes, they began to drop back behind me into the night.

The moment I noticed that, I dropped Roanoke back to his trot. Galloping was not to his taste, but he could swing on at close to full speed with that shambling trot of his and keep it up forever. It did not take long. The hunt faded behind me. The yelling began to grow musical with the distance; and finally it died away—first to an occasional obscure murmur in the wind, and then to nothing.

I think we did thirty miles before the morning was on us. Then I put up and spent another hungry day in a clump of trees. But food for Roanoke, not for me, was the main thing at that time. When the day ended, I sent that old veteran out to travel again, and we were soon in the mountains, soon climbing slowly, soon winding and weaving ourselves up to cloud level.

Until I got to that height, back in my own country, I did not realize how frightened I had been. But now that the mischief was behind me, I felt fairly groggy. I sent one bullet through a pair of fool jack rabbits sitting side by side, the next morning, behind a rock. They barely made a meal for me. I could have eaten a hindquarter of an ox, I was so hungry. I kept poor Roanoke drudging away until about noon. Then I made camp and spent thirty-six hours without moving.

I always do that after a hard march, if I can. It is always best to work hard while there's the least hint of trouble in the offing, but when the wind lets up, I don't know of a better way to insure long life and happiness than by resting a lot. I was like a sponge. I could work for a hundred hours without closing my eyes; but at the end of that time, I could sleep two days, solid, with just enough waking time to cook and eat one meal on each of those days.

Roanoke was a good deal the same way. We spent a day and a half in a sort of stupor, but the result was that when we *did* start on, I had under me an animal that wasn't half fagged and ready to be beaten, but a mule with his ears up and quivering; and my own head was rested and prepared for trouble.

I hit for my old camping ground—not any particular section, though I knew every inch of the high range, by this time—the whole wide region above timberline—a bitter, naked, cheerless country, in lots of ways, but a safe one. For seven years, safety had to take the place of home and friends for me.

An infernal north wind began to shriek among the peaks as soon as I got up there among them. But I didn't budge for ten wretched days or more. I spent a shuddering, miserable existence. There is nothing on earth that comes so close to above timberline for real hell!

I've heard naturalists talk about the beauties of insects and birds and whatnot above the place where the trees stop growing. Well, I can't agree with them. Perhaps I haven't a soul. But those high places make me pretty sick! When I see the long, dark line of trees end, that cuts in and out among the mountains like the mark of high water, it sends a chill through me.

But for seven years I had spent the bulk of my life in that horrible part of the world. Seven years—eighteen to twenty-five! Every year before twenty-five is twice as long as every year after that time.

Well, I stayed in the old safe level, as I have said, about ten days. Then I dropped Roanoke five thousand feet nearer to civilization and stopped, one day, on the edge of a little town—right out between two hills where there was a little shack of a cabin standing. I knew that cabin, and I knew that the man inside it ought to know me.

I had stayed over with him half a dozen nights, and every time I used his house as a hotel, he got ten or twenty dollars out of me. Because that was one of the rules of the game. If a long rider struck up an acquaintanceship with one of the mountaineers, he always had to pay for it through the nose in the end.

However, I couldn't be sure that the old man Sargent hadn't changed his mind about me. I left Roanoke fidgeting among the trees on the hillside, for he could smell the sweet hay from the barn at that distance, and his mouth was watering. Then I slid down the hill and peeked through the windows. Everything seemed as cheerful and dirty and careless as ever.

Sargent had two grown-up sons. The three of them put in their time on a place where there wasn't work enough to keep one respectable two-handed man busy. There wasn't more than enough money for one man, if he wanted to be civilized. But civilization didn't harmonize with the Sargents. They wanted to live easy, even if they had to live low.

When I saw that there wasn't any change in them, I took Roanoke to the barn and put him up where he could eat all the hay he wanted. Because you can trust a mule to stop before the danger mark—which is a trust that you can't put in a horse.

Then I went to the house, and the three of them gave me a pretty snug welcome. Old man Sargent insisted that I take the best chair—his own chair. He insisted, too, that I have something to eat. I had had enough for breakfast to last a couple of days, but I let out a link and laid into some mighty good corn bread and molasses that he dished up to me along with some coffee so strong that it would of taken the bristles off of pigskin.

I said: "How long ago did you make this coffee, Sargent?"

"I dunno," said he.

"He swabs out the pot once a month," said one of the boys, grinning, "and the rest of the time, he just keeps changing the brew a little! A little more water —a little more coffee!"

Well, it tasted like that, sort of generally bad and strong—mighty strong.

I put away half a cup, just enough to moisten the corn bread that I swallowed.

"Have you come down to get Dinsmore?" said Bert Sargent.

The name hit the button, of course, and I turned around and stared at him.

"Why, Dinsmore has been setting waiting down in Elmira for three days!" said old man Sargent.

"Waiting for what?" said I. "I've been up in the mountains, and I haven't heard."

Of course, they were glad enough to tell. Bad news for anyone else was good news for those rascals. It seems that Dinsmore had appeared, suddenly, in the streets of Elmira. At noonday. That was his way of doing things—with a high hand—acting as though there were no reason in the world why he should expect trouble from anyone. He went to the bulletin board beside the post office and there he posted up a big notice. He had the roll of paper under his arm, and he tacked it up with plenty of nails, not caring what other signs he covered.

Well, sir, the reading of that sign was something like this:

"Attention, Leon Porfilo! I want you, not the twenty thousand. If you want *me,* you can expect that I'll be ready for you any day between three and four if you'll ride through Main Street. I'll let you know which way to shoot!

Jeffrey Dinsmore

I don't mean to say that the Sargent family told me this story with so little detail. What they did do, however, was to give me all the facts, among the three of them. When I had sifted those facts over in my mind, I stood up. I was so worried that I didn't care if they saw the trouble in my face.

"You don't like this news so well as you might,

partner?" says old Sargent very smooth and swallowing a grin.

I looked down at that wicked old loafer and hated him with all my heart.

"I don't like that news at all," I admitted.

The three of them exclaimed all in a breath with delight. They couldn't help it. Then I told them that I was tired, and they showed me to a mattress on the floor of the next room. I lay there for a time trying to think out what I should do, and all the time I could hear the malicious whispers of the three in the kitchen. They were discussing with vile pleasure the shock that had appeared in my face when I had been told the news. They were like vultures, that trio.

Well, I was tired enough to go to sleep anyway, after a time. Then I wakened with a start and found that it was daylight. That was what you might call a real hundred-per-cent sleep. I felt better, of course, when I got up in the morning, and in the kitchen I found old man Sargent with his greasy hair tumbling down over his face and his face as lined and shadowed as though he had been drinking whisky all the night. I suppose that really low thoughts tear up a man's body as much as the booze.

He gave a side look as sharp as a bird's to see if there was still any trouble in my eyes, but I put on a mask for him and came out into the kitchen singing. All at once, a sort of horror at that old man and at the life I had been leading came over me.

I hurried out of the house and down to the creek. Of course it was ice cold, but I needed a bath, inside and out, I felt. I stripped and dived and climbed back onto the creek bank with enough shivers running up and down my spine to have done for a whole school of minnows.

But I felt better. A lot better.

When I went back to the house for breakfast, I saw that one of the two boys was not on hand, and I asked where he was. His father said that he had gone off to try to get a deer, but that sounded like a queer excuse to me. I couldn't imagine a Sargent doing such a thing as this, at this hour in the morning! I began to grow a little uneasy—I didn't exactly know why!

After breakfast, as I left, I offered the old rat a twenty-dollar bill, and he took it and spread it out with a real gulp of joy. Cash came very seldom into his life.

"But," said he at last, peering at me hopefully and making his voice a wheedling drawl, "ain't I give you extra important news, this trip? Ain't it worth a mite more?"

I was too disgusted to answer. I turned on my heel and left, and as I went out, I could hear him snarling covertly behind me.

## ··· 17 ···

However, I didn't like to fall out with the Sargents. I knew that they were swine, but, after all, I might need their help pretty early and pretty often in the next few years of my life.

I went out to Roanoke and sat in the manger in front of him, thinking, or trying to think, while the old rascal started biting at me as though he were going to make breakfast off me. I decided, finally, that the only thing for me was to head straight for Elmira and take my chances there, because if I didn't meet Dinsmore right away, my name would be pretty worthless through the mountains. Besides, it was the very thing I had wanted.

But I had never dreamed of a fight in a town—and a big town like Elmira, that had a four-story hotel, and a regular business section, and four streets going north and south and four streets going east and west. There were as many as fifteen hundred people in Elmira, I suppose.

It was a regular city, and it seemed a good deal like craziness to try to stage a fight in such a place. As well start a chicken fight in the midst of a gang of rattlesnakes. No matter which of us won, he was sure to be nabbed by the local police right after the fight.

I wondered what could be in the head of Dinsmore, unless he had an arrangement with the sheriff of that county to turn him loose, in case he were the man who won the fight. I decided that this must be the fact, and that worried me more than ever. However, there wasn't much that I could do except to ride in and take my chance with Dinsmore. But one of the bad features was that I had never seen Dinsmore, whereas everyone had had a thousand looks at me in the posters which offered a reward for my capture.

Well, I saddled Roanoke and started down the Elmira trail. The first cross trail I came to, there I saw a board nailed on the side of a fence post and on the board there was all spread out a pretty good poster which said:

### DINSMORE—TWENTY THOUSAND DOLLARS' REWARD

I made Roanoke jump for the sign to see the face in detail. It was rather a small photograph, but it was a very clear one, and I was fairly staggered when I leaned over and found myself looking into the eyes of the very same fellow who had climbed the back fence of the governor's house a second before me on that rousing night in the capital city.

So that was Dinsmore!

It wasn't a very hot day, but I jumped out of the saddle and sat down under a tree and smoked a cigarette and fanned myself and did some very tall damning.

It was all a confusing and nasty mess, of course. A *mighty* nasty mess! I hardly dared to think out all of the ideas that jumped into my mind. There had been the anger of the governor when I mentioned the name of Dinsmore. There had been a sort of savage satisfaction when I suggested that the other outlaw and I shoot it out for the pardon. That, together with the unknown presence of Dinsmore at the house—and the pretty face of the governor's wife—well, I was fairly done up at the thought, you may be sure.

I could remember, too, that Dinsmore, though he had always been a fighting man, had never been a complete devil until about a year before—which was about the date of the governor's marriage.

I don't mean to say that I immediately jumped to a lot of nasty conclusions. But a great many doubts and suspicions were floating through the back of my brain. I didn't want to believe a single one of them. But what could I do?

The first thing was to throw myself on the back of Roanoke and go down that hillside like a snowslide well underway. Blindly as a slide, too, and the result was that as I dipped out of the trees and came into the sunny little open valley below, I got two rifle shots squarely at my face. I didn't try to turn Roanoke aside. I just jammed him across that clearing with the spurs hanging in his flanks, and I opened fire with both revolvers as I went, firing as fast as I could and just in a general direction, of course!

Well, I got results. Snapshooting is always a good deal of a chance. This snapshooting into the blind brush got me a yelp of pain that meant a hit and was followed by a groan that meant a *bad* hit.

After that, there was a considerable crashing through the brush, and I made out at least three horses smearing their way off through the underbrush. But what mostly interested me was that the groaning remained just as near and just as heavy as before. So I went in search of it, and when I came to the place, I found a long fellow in ragged clothes lying on his face behind a shrub. I turned him over and with one look at his yellow face I knew that he was dying.

It was young Marcus Sargent.

Of course I knew at once why he had been missing at the breakfast table. They guessed that I would head straight for Elmira now that I had the news. So young Marcus thought of the twenty thousand dollars and decided that there was no reason why he should not dip his hands into the reward!

He wasn't a coward. He was in such pain that it changed his color, but it didn't keep him from sneering at me in hate. When you wrong a man, hate always comes out of it—on your side.

But I didn't hate him, in turn. I merely thanked heaven that he had missed; and I didn't see how he had, because I'd watched him ring down a squirrel out of a treetop many a time.

"How did you happen to miss?" I asked him. "Hand shake, Mark?"

The first thing he answered was: "Am I done for?"

I answered him brutally enough: "You're done for. You can't live two minutes, I suppose; that slug went through you in the spot where it would do me the most good!"

"You're a lucky swine!" said Marcus. "Well, anyway, I dunno that life is so sweet that I hate the leavin' of it. But over in Elmira—if you should happen to run across Sue Hunter, hand her my watch, will you? Tell her it's from me. You'll know her by her picture inside the cover."

I hated nothing in the world more than touching that

watch. But I did it, at last, and dropped it into my pocket.

He didn't want to die before he had done as much harm as he could. He turned on his own family, saying: "It wasn't me alone. The whole three of us talked it over last night!"

"Look here, Mark," said I, getting a little sick as I watched his color change, "is there anything I can do to make you more comfortable?"

"Sure," said he. "Lend me a chaw, will you?"

I didn't chew tobacco, and I told him that I had none for him.

"Well," said he, "then fetch me my own plug out of my hip pocket, will you?"

But before I could get it for him, he was dead.

I didn't like this affair for a lot of reasons. In the first place, I've never sunk lead in a man without hating the job. Though I've had the necessity or the bad luck of having to kill ten times my share of men, there was never a time when I didn't loathe it, and loathe the thought of it afterward.

But that was only half of the reason that I disliked this ugly little adventure in the hollow. I had a fair idea that the two or three curs who had ambushed me with young Sargent would now ride for Elmira full tilt and tell the sheriff of what they had tried to do and of where they had last seen me. So, in two or three hours, the sheriff might be setting a fine trap for me in the town.

Of course, I only needed a moment of thought to see that that was a foolish idea. No matter how little the people esteemed me, they would not think me such a perfect idiot as to ride on toward the town after I knew that a warning was speeding toward it in the form of three messengers.

No, the sheriff was really not very apt to lay a plot

for me in the town. Rather, he was pretty sure to come foaming down to the place I had been seen and try to follow my trail from that point.

Well, I decided that if that were the case, he could pick up my trail if he cared to and follow it right back to his own home town.

In short, my idea was that when people heard I had appeared so close to Elmira, every gun-wearing citizen would take a turn on his fastest horse and treat himself to a holiday hunting down twenty thousand dollars' worth of "critter."

I believed that that town would be well cleaned out and that the best thing I could do was to drive straight for Elmira itself, simply swinging a little wide off the main trail. Perhaps nine tenths of the fighting men would be out hunting me when I reached Elmira, hunting Jeffrey Dinsmore!

Jeffrey Dinsmore, slender and delicately made, and as handsome for a man as the governor's wife was lovely for a girl! Thinking of her and of Dinsmore, I could understand why it was that Mike O'Rourke was only pretty and not truly beautiful. Molly might grow plain enough in the face in another ten years, but the governor's wife was another matter. She would simply become charming in new ways as time passed over her head.

There was something magnificent and removed and different about her. She was the sort of a person I wondered any man could ever have the courage to love— she seemed so mighty superior to me! Well, you can guess from all of this that I wasn't in the most cheerful frame of mind in the world until, about two hours afterward, I looked through a gap in the trees and the brush, and I saw about a hundred men piling down the hillside in just the opposite direction and knew that I had guessed right!

## ··· 18 ···

Elmira had turned out its best and bravest to swarm out to the place where my trail had been found and lost by those three heroes who accompanied young Mark Sargent. They had a long ride before them, and no matter how fast they spurred back toward Elmira, they were not apt to arrive there until many hours after I had passed through. My chief concern now was simply lest there still remained too many fighting men in the town. But I was not greatly worried about that.

I felt that I had reduced the dangers of Elmira to a very small point. The danger which remained was from Dinsmore alone.

How great that danger was I could not really guess. It was true that he established a great reputation for himself in Texas, but before this I had met with men of a great repute in distant sections of the country, and they had proved not so deadly on a closer knowing.

Furthermore, when one has picked up another man
and dropped him on the pavement, one is not apt to
respect his prowess greatly. Which may explain fairly
thoroughly why I thought that I could handle Mr.
Dinsmore with ease.

I did not think, however, that he would be prepared
for me in Elmira. I thought that I probably would be
permitted to canter down the street unobserved by Mr.
Dinsmore; because if the entire town was so busy hunting me, it seemed illogical that I should drop into Elmira.

I expected to canter easily through the town, with
only the danger of some belated storekeeper or some
old man seeing and knowing me, for the rest of the
town seemed to be out in the saddle.

Of course, I hoped that Dinsmore would not be on
hand, because after I had answered his first invitation
and he failed to appear, it would be my turn to lead,
and I could request him to appear at a place of my
own selection. The advantage would then be all on my
side.

Outside of the town I stopped for a time. I let the
mule rest, and I took it easy myself. I had a few hours
on my hands before the appointed time to show myself to little Dinsmore in the town.

However, though Roanoke rested well enough, I
cannot say that my nerves were very easy. The time
was coming closer, faster than any express train I ever
watched in my life. The waiting was the strain. Whereas Dinsmore, knowing that the fight might come any
day, paid no heed, but could maintain a leisurely look-
out—or none at all!

A pair of eternities went by at last, however. Then I
swung onto Roanoke and started him into the town.
Everything went on about as I had expected it. The

town was emptied of men. The first I saw was an old octogenarian with his trousers patched with a piece of old sack.

The poor old man looked more than half dead, and probably was. He didn't lift his head from his hobble as I rattled by. The first bit of danger that came into my way was signaled by the screaming voice of a woman.

"There goes Leon Porfilo! There'll be a murder in this town today!"

It wasn't a very cheerful reception, take it all in all. But I pulled Roanoke back to an easy trot, and then I took him down to a walk, because I saw that I was coming pretty close to the place of the rendezvous. When I passed that place—though I wanted most terribly to pass it fast!—still I had to be at a gait from which a man can shoot straight—and I've never yet seen anyone but a liar that could come near to accuracy from a trot or a gallop. Try it yourself—especially with a revolver—and see what happens. Even a walking horse is bad enough. It's hard when the target is moving; it's a lot harder when the shooter is in motion.

So I steeled myself as well as I could and reached a sort of mental bucket down into the innards of myself and drew up all the champagne that there was in me. I mustered a smile. Smiling helps a fellow, somehow. I don't mean in any fool way like they have it in rag-time songs and old proverbs. But smiling makes your gun hand steady.

Pretty soon I was right in the midst of the place where danger was to come at me, according to the warning that Dinsmore had sent out. I began to think that the whole thing was just a great bluff and that nothing would come out of it! It was a big play on the part of Dinsmore, and he hadn't the least idea of living up to his promise.

Just as this thought struck me, I heard a calm, smooth voice call out behind me: "Well, Porfilo?"

It was the sort of a voice that comes from a man who doesn't want to call any public attention to himself. He aims to reach just the ear of the man to whom he is speaking. But, at the same time, I knew that that was the voice of Dinsmore, and I knew that Dinsmore was mighty bad medicine; and I knew that the fight of my life was on my hands.

I spun about in the saddle with the gun in my hand —and I saw that he had not even drawn his weapon!

The shock of it sickened me. I couldn't keep from shooting—I was so thoroughly set for that pull of the trigger—but I did manage to shoot wide of the mark. Just as the gun exploded, I saw my new friend Dinsmore make as pretty a draw as I have ever had the pleasure of witnessing. One of those snap movements that jump a gun out of the leather and shoot it from the hip.

In the meantime, I jerked my own gun back and fired again, but my hand was mighty uncertain. The whole affair was so infernally unnerving that I was not myself. The idea that any man in the world would dare to stand up to me and give me the first chance at a draw was too much for me!

I got in my second shot before he fired his first, but all I did with that second bullet was to break a grocery-store window! Then a thunderbolt clipped me along the head and knocked me back in the saddle.

I was completely out—as perfectly out as though a hammer had landed on me—but it happened that in falling, my weight was thrown squarely forward, and my arms dangled around the neck of Roanoke. He started the same instant, I suppose, with that shambling, ridiculously smooth trot of his; so that I was able to stick to his back.

I think that the wild yelling of old men, and women, and children was what brought me back to my senses. Or partially back to them, for my head was spinning and crimson was running over my eyes. However, I was able to sit straighter in the saddle and put Roanoke into a gallop.

I was a dead man, of course. I learned afterward about the miracle that saved me. For the gun of that great expert, that famous Dinsmore, failed to work. The cylinder stuck on the next shot, and before he could get the other gun out to blow me out of this life and into limbo, that wise-headed mule of mine had put a buckboard at the side of the street between himself and that gunman.

Dinsmore had to run out into the middle of the street to get the next shot. But when he saw me again, I suppose that the distance was getting too great for accurate work even for him, and besides, Roanoke was shooting me along under the shadow of the trees.

At any rate, there he stood in a raging passion and emptied that second gun of his without putting a mark upon either the mule or the mule's rider. I suppose there is no doubt that the fury of that little man was what saved me more than anything else.

But presently I was blinking at the sun like a person wakened out of a dream, and behind me lay Elmira in a hollow; and up and down my head ran a pain like the agony of a cutting knife through tender flesh; and down in Elmira was a man who was telling the world that the "coward had run away from him!"

I should like to be able to say that, halting only to tie a sleeve of my shirt around my head, I turned and whirled back into Elmira to find him again. But I have to confess that nothing could have induced me to face that calm little devil of a mankiller on that day. For the moment, I felt that I could *never* have the courage to fight or face him again! I felt that I would take water sooner.

First of all, I found a little hollow about ten miles back among the hills, and there I made myself comfortable, heated some water, washed out my wound, and bound it up. Then I rode straight on to the next little village. On the way, I had to duck three or four parties of manhunters. I didn't have to ask who they were hunting for. I simply wanted to dodge them and get on, for I knew that they wanted either Dinsmore or me.

The next town had not much more than an ugly look, a hotel, and half a dozen shacks. But in one of these shacks was an old doctor, and that was what I wanted. The new-fangled ideas had taken his trade away from him. But he was good enough for me, on that day.

I left Roanoke behind his house and went to the back window and saw the poor old man sitting there in a kitchen that was blackened with the shadows of the trees that hung over the place—blackened with time, too, if you can understand what I mean by that. I pitied him, suddenly, so much that I almost forgot the pain in my head. Young men are like that.

They pity almost everyone except themselves. I never ride through a village without wondering how people can live in it. Yet I suppose that every one of them is prettier than my home town of Mendez.

I went in, and the doctor looked sidewise from his whittling of a stick and then back to it.

"Well, Porfilo," said he, "I been hearin' that you got licked, at last! And a little feller did it! Well, for some things bigness ain't needed."

He stood up—about five feet in his total height. I

hung above him, ducking my head to keep from scraping the cobwebs off the rafters.

"I've got my head sliced open. Sew me up, pop," said I.

"Set down and rest yourself, son," said he. "I see you got sense enough to let little men fix you *up,* anyway!"

## · · · 19 · · ·

I listened to him mumbling and muttering to himself, while I set my teeth and snarled at the pain, until the job was done and my head washed and bandage arranged around it. He gave me a lot of extra bandage, and a salve, and he asked me if I had a good mirror so that I could watch the wound every day. I told him that I had, and asked him what the price would be.

"If you're flat busted, the way most of your kind always are," said he, "there ain't no charge, except for your good will. Besides, any young feller has got a reward comin' to him when he listens to an old goat like me chatterin' for a while. But if you're flush, well, for bandagin' the head of an outlaw and a mankiller like you—well, it's worth about—thirty dollars, I reckon!"

I sifted a hundred dollars out of my wallet and put it in his hand.

I was out of the door before he had counted it over and he shouted: "Hey, you—"

I was on Roanoke, with that fine old fellow standing in the doorway and shouting: "Come back here! You give me too much."

I sent Roanoke on his way, and the last I saw of him, that poor old man was running and stumbling and staggering after me, waving his glasses in one hand and his money in the other hand and telling me to come back. But I only saw him for a moment. Then I was away among the trees, with Roanoke climbing steadily.

I kept him south through the highlands. When I was far enough away from the last trouble, I made small marches every day, because I knew that a wound won't heal quickly so long as a man is running about too much. While I was lazying around, I worked until both wrists ached over my guns. Because there was fear in me—real fear in me! I had gone for seven years from one fight to another, never beaten, always the conqueror. Now a little fellow had blown me off my pedestal!

I had to get ready to fight him again. I knew that, and I can't tell you that I didn't relish the knowing. In the meantime I had to get in touch with Mike. For she would think, as probably everyone in the mountains thought, that I had either been killed by the aftereffects of that wound in the head received from Jeffrey Dinsmore, or else that I had been so thoroughly broken in spirit as a result of that first defeat that I had shrunk away to a new land and dared not show myself in my old haunts.

Well, I thought of a letter, first of all; but then I decided that it would be better to see her, because it might be the very last time that I should ever see her in this world. For, having once witnessed the gun play

of Jeffrey Dinsmore, I knew that at the best I would
need a touch of good fortune in order to beat him in a
fair gunfight. What with my bulk and my experience,
how could I challenge him with any other weapon?

So I drifted farther south through the mountains until I came one midnight to the O'Rourke house and
stood underneath the black front of the house—all
black, except for a single light in the window of Mike.

I called her with a whistle which was a seven-year-
old signal between us. She did not open the door and
first look down at me, but she came flying down the
stairs and then out the front door and down the steps
and into my arms. But, when she had made sure that
it was I, she stood back from me and laughed and
nodded with her happiness. She told me that she had
been sure that I was dead, in spite of other rumors.

"What sort of talk has been going around about
me, then?" I asked her.

She shook her head. But I told her that I would
have to have it.

"They are fools," said she, but there was a strain
in her voice. "They say that you are afraid to go back
and face Dinsmore!"

Well, I *was* afraid. So I blurted out: "I *am* afraid,
Mike."

I saw it take her breath, and I saw her flinch from
me. Then she answered very calmly: "However, you'll
go back and fight him again!"

I was mighty proud of her. You don't find women
who will talk like that very often. But Mike was the
truest mountain-bred kind—thoroughbred, in her own
way. I spent a single hour with her there in the garden. Then I told her that I was starting back.

"North?" asked Mike.

"North, of course," said I. "You don't think that I'll
try to dodge a second meeting?"

"Of *course* I didn't think so!" said she. However, I could feel the relief in her voice. She began to pat the neck of old Roanoke.

"Roanoke," said she, "bring him back safe to me!" So I left Mike and rode north again.

It was a hard journey. I had gone for seven years more or less paying no attention to decent precautions, because they had not been so necessary to me. In fact, I had not appreciated the change in my affairs until I started that northward journey again.

It began in the first house where I put up for a night. Old Marshall's house was a pretty frequent stopping place for me. His family had taken a good deal of money out of my hand, and more than that, his nephew, who ran the little bit of cattle land the old man owned, seemed to respect me and to like me, because he was always trying to find a better chance to talk to me.

But when I came to the house this night, everyone merely stared at me, at first, and then I could hear them whispering and even chuckling behind their hands. People had not done that to me since I was a little boy in school. It made my heart cold, and then it made my heart hot.

But I waited until something came out. With people like that, nothing could be left to silence very long. They had to bring out what they thought and put it into words.

So big Dick Marshall, the nephew, came and lounged against the wall near my chair.

"We hear that you been having your own sorts of trouble?" said he.

I lifted the bandage which I still wore, and showed him the scar.

"I was nipped," said I.

He laughed in my face. "You didn't go back for any more of *that* medicine, I guess?" said he.

I wanted to knock him down. But after a moment I decided that there was no use in doing that. Because he was not a bad fellow. Just a clod. No more cruel than a bull in a herd—and no less.

That, and the mischievous, contemptuous smile with which he watched me out of sight the next morning, as I rode away, should have convinced me, I suppose, that there was worse trouble ahead. But when I really found it out, it was merely because four young fellows came bang—over a hilltop behind me and tried to ride me down in the next hollow. When they saw that I was making time away from them to the tree line, they opened fire at me.

When I got to the trees, I told myself that I was all right, but to my real astonishment, just as I drew up on the rein and brought Roanoke back to a walk, I heard the whole four of them crashing through the underbrush!

I sent Roanoke ahead again, full steam. He was as smooth a worker as a snake through the shrubbery, and the four began to fall behind. I could hear them yelling with rage as they judged, by the noise, that they were losing ground behind me. But all the time I was thinking hard and fast. It wasn't right. Four youngsters like these, not one of whom had probably ever pulled a gun on another man, should not be riding behind Leon Porfilo. By no means!

Well, I decided to find out what the reason was. So I cut back through the forest. The trees were pretty dense, and so I was able to get right in behind the party. I sighted them and found them just as I wanted to find them. They were strung out by the heat of the work, and one fellow was lagging far behind with a lame horse.

He had no eyes for the back trail, and he could hear no sound behind him, he was so eager to get ahead. It was easy enough to slip along in a dark hollow and stick a gun in the small of his back. I clapped my hand over his mouth so that I stifled his yell. Then I turned him around and looked him over. He was just a baby. About eighteen or nineteen, with big, pale-blue eyes, and a foolish sort of a smile trembling on his mouth.

He was afraid. But he was not afraid as much as he should have been at meeting Leon Porfilo. This may sound pretty fat-headed, but you have to understand that I had been the pet dragon around those parts for the past seven years, and I wasn't in the habit of having infants like this boy on my trail!

I said to him: "Son, do you know who I am?"

"You're Porfilo!" said he.

"Then what in the devil do you mean by riding so hard down my trail?"

He looked straight back at me. "There's twenty thousand dollars' worth of reasons," said he, as bold as you please.

"Is it a very safe business?" said I.

He wouldn't answer, but those big pale eyes of his didn't waver.

"You can do what you want," said he. "I didn't have no fair chance—with you sneakin' up behind like that. No matter what happens, my brother'll get you after I'm dead!"

"Am I to murder you?" said I.

"You don't dare to leave me on your trail!" said he.

Well, it sickened me, and that was all there was to it! He actually wanted to fight the thing out with me, I think.

"You're loose!" said I, and dropped my gun back in the holster.

He jerked his horse back and grabbed for his own gun. Then he saw that  I was making no move toward mine, and so he began to gape at me as though he were seeing double. Finally he disappeared in the trees. But it's a fact that I couldn't have fired a shot at that little fool.

This thing, and the talk of young Marshall, showed me how far I had dropped in the estimation of the mountain men since they had heard that little Dinsmore beat me in a fair fight. I knew that I would be in frightful danger from that moment on.

## ••• 20 •••

I knew that there was danger because my cloak of invincibility was quite thrown away. For seven years I had paraded up and down through the mountains, and men had not dared to go out to hunt me except when they had celebrated leaders to show them the way, and when they had prepared carefully organized bands of hard fighters and straight shooters.

It had been easy enough to get out of the reach of these large parties. But when the hills were beginning to buzz with the doings of little groups of from three to five manhunters—well, then my danger was multiplied by a thousand. Multiplied most of all, however, by the mental attitude of the people who rode out against me.

For there's only one reason that so many straight-shooting frontiersmen fail when they come to take a shot at a so-called desperado. That reason is that their nerve fails them. They are not sure of themselves. So their rifles miss, and the desperado who has all the confidence that they lack does prodigious things. One hears, here and there, of terrible warriors who have dropped half a dozen men, and gotten off unhurt!

Of course, I was never on a par with these. In fact, my principle was not to shoot to kill unless I had a known scoundrel up against me. But now I felt that my back was against the wall.

There was only one solution for me, and that was to get at Dinsmore as soon as possible and fight it out with him, and by his death put an end to the careless- ness of the fools who were hounding me through the hills. But in the meantime, how was I to get at Dins- more himself?

I decided that I must try the very scheme which he had tried on me. I must send him a message and a challenge in the message to meet me at a place and a time of my own choosing. Two days later chance threw a messenger into my path.

I was in a tangle of shrubs on the shoulder of a mountain with Roanoke on the other side, his saddle off, rolling to freshen himself, and playing like a colt, as only a mule, among grown animals, likes to play. While I sat on a rock at the edge of the brush, I saw a pair of horsemen and then a third working up the trail straight toward me.

I was in no hurry. This was rough country of my own choosing, and Roanoke could step away from any horse in the world, in that sort of going, like a moun- tain sheep! I simply got out my glasses and studied the three. As they came closer, rising deeper into the field of the glass, I thought that I could guess what they were —three headhunters, and mine was the head that they wanted.

For they were too well mounted to be just casual cowpunchers. Every man was literally armed to the teeth. I saw sheathed rifles under their right knees. I saw a pair of revolvers at their hips. One fellow had another pair of six-shooters in his saddle holsters. They looked as though they were a detail from an army!

I went across the knob of the shoulder of that mountain and I saddled Roanoke. But I didn't like to leave that place. I was irritated again. Four youngsters had been out hunting me the last time. Now it was three grown men! Three!

You might say that my pride was offended, because that was exactly the case!

I ended by dropping the reins of Roanoke, and the wise old mule stood as still as death in the shadow of the trees, flopping his ears back and forth at me, but not so much as switching his tail to knock away the flies that were settling on his flanks and biting deep as only mountain flies know how to bite!

I have always thought that Roanoke knew when there was trouble coming, and that he enjoyed the prospect of it with all his heart. There was faith and strength and courage in the nature of that brute, but I am sure that there was a good deal of the devil in him, too!

I left him behind and started down among the rocks until I found exactly the sort of a place that I wanted, a regular nest, with plenty of chances to look out from it with a rifle. I had a fine rifle with me, and ready for action. As for my humor, it was nearer to killing than it had ever been in my life.

The three came up with surprising speed, and I knew by that that they were well mounted. As they came, I could hear their voices rising up to me like echoes up a well shaft. These voices, and that laughter, was sometimes dim, sometimes loud and crackling in my ear. Because in the mountains, where the air is very thin, sound travels not so freshly and easily. The least blow of wind may turn a shout into a whisper.

Have you never noticed that mountaineers, when they come down toward sea level, are a noisy lot?

I could hear all the talk of the three, and by their very talk I could judge that they were in the best of spirits.

Then: "Will you keep that darn bay from joggin' around and tryin' to turn around in the trail, Baldy?"

"It ain't me. It's the hoss. It wants to get back to that stable—"

"A hired hoss," said a third voice, "is something that I ain't never rode."

They came suddenly around the next bend of the trail, and I barely had the time to duck down in my nest of rocks. I had thought them at least fifty yards farther away from that bend!

I was not quite in time, at that.

"Hey!" yelled the first man—he of the bay horse.

"Well?" growled one of the others.

"Something in those rocks—"

"Maybe it's Porfilo!" laughed another.

"That's the gent you want!"

"Just run up to them rocks and ask him to step out and have it out with you, Baldy!"

Baldy said apologetically: "Well, I can't keep you from laughing. But I would of said that the brim of a sombrero—"

I took off my hat and prepared my rifle. As I freshened my grip on it and tickled the trigger with my forefinger, I have to admit that I was ready to kill. I was hot and sore to the very bone. They came laughing and joking on my trail. It was a vacation, a regular party to them!

As they came closer, as the nodding shadow of the

bay appeared on the white trail just before my nest, I stood up with the rifle at my shoulder.

There's something discouraging about a rifle. About ten times as much can be said with a rifle as can be said with even a pair of revolvers. The revolvers may have a lot of speed and lead in 'em. But they *might* miss—they're pretty *apt* to miss. Even a coward will take a gambling chance now and then. But when a rifle in a steady hand is looking in your direction, you feel sure that something is bound to drop. Somehow, there is an instinct in men which makes everyone think that the muzzle is pointed directly at him.

Only one of the three made a pass at a gun. The two boys behind shoved their hands in the air right pronto. But Baldy, up in the lead, passed a hand toward his off Colt. He was within the tenth part of a second of his long sleep when he did that. I think that there must be something in mental telepathy, because the moment that thought to kill came into my mind, he stuck both of his paws into the air and kept his arms stiff.

His bay turned around as if it were on a pivot and started moving back down the trail.

"Take your left hand, Baldy," said I, "and stop that horse pronto!"

He did exactly as I told him to do.

"Now, boys," said I, stepping out from the rocks with that rifle only at the ready, "I suppose that you recognize me. I'm Leon Porfilo. If you want to know me any better, make a pass at a holster. You, Baldy, were about half a step from purgatory a minute ago. The rest of you, turn your horses around with your knees. If you're not riding hired horses, they ought to do that much without feeling the bit. Turn your horses around. I like the looks of your backs better than your faces."

There was not a word of answer. They turned their

nags obediently around. There they sat with five arms sticking into the air.

I made them dismount—the rear pair. Then I made them back up until they were near me. After that, I took their hands behind them and tied cords over them—tied them until they groaned.

"You pair of sapheads!" said I. "Sit down over there by that rock, will you—and don't make any noise—because I feel restless today. I feel mighty restless. Baldy, you're next!"

I tied Baldy with his own lariat, and I tied him well. I tied his hands tight behind him, and I tied his feet together under the belly of the bay.

Then I took an old envelope and wrote big on it:

To everybody in general, and Dinsmore in particular: Dinsmore got the drop on me in Elmira. I want to find him. I ask him to come and find me, now. I'll meet him any afternoon between three and four in the Elmira Pass. This holds good for the next month.

Leon Porfilo

I pinned that on the back of Baldy. Then I turned him loose. All that I wanted was to have the world see my message back to Dinsmore to let them know that I was waiting for him.

How that bay did sprint down the hill! There was a puff of trail dust, you might say, and then the bay and Baldy landed in the hollow of the valley below the mountain, and after that, they skimmed up the mountain on the other side. The bay was certainly signaling that he intended to get to that stable!

Then I went back to the other two. I didn't say a great deal, but they seemed to think that it was worth listening to. I told them that I had gone for seven years, letting people hound me through the mountains and not shooting back.

I told them that my next job was to find Dinsmore and kill him, but that in the meantime I intended to shoot, and to shoot to kill! If I met the pair of them again, they were dead men—on the street or in the mountains—it made no difference to me!

I think those fellows took it to heart. Then, because I hadn't the slightest fear that they would overtake the bay, I untied their hands and let them mount and ride back the way that they came.

# ··· 21 ···

All in all, I thought that this move of mine was a clever one and that it would reestablish me a great deal through the mountains; but the answer of Jeffrey Dinsmore was a crushing blow, because that rascal went into the office of the biggest newspaper in the capital city ten days later and called on the editor and introduced himself, and allowed the editor to photograph him, and dictated to the editor a long statement about various things.

It was a grand thing in the way of a scoop for that paper. I saw a copy of it and there were headlines across the front page three inches deep. Most of the rest of the front page was covered with pictures of the editor, and the editor's office where the terrible Dinsmore had appeared; and, in the center, surrounded with little pen sketches of Dinsmore in the act of shooting down a dozen men in various scenes, was a picture of Jeffrey—the picture which the editor had snapped of him.

It showed him, dapper and easy and smiling, smoking a cigar, and holding it up so that the camera could catch the name on it. That was a cigar which the editor, mentioning the fact proudly in his article, declared that he had given to the desperado.

Altogether, it was a great spread for Dinsmore, and the editor, and the newspaper, and a great fall for me. I understood afterward that the editor got three offers from other newspapers immediately afterward, and that his salary was doubled to keep him where he was.

He couldn't say too much about the affair.

Dinsmore had appeared through the window of his office, four stories above the street, at nine o'clock in the evening when most of the reporters were out at work on their stories and their copy. The editor of *The Eagle,* being busy at his desk, looked up just in time to see a dapper young man sliding through the window with a revolver pointed at the editorial head and the smiling face of Mr. Dinsmore behind the revolver.

So the editor, taking great pride in the fact that he did not put his hands into the air, turned around and from his tilted swivel chair asked Dinsmore what he would have.

"A good reputation!" said Dinsmore.

"From that point on," declared the editor in his article, "we got on very well together, because there is nothing like a good laugh to start an interview smoothly!"

They talked of a great many things. That editor's account of Dinsmore, his polished manners, his amiable smile, was so pleasant that it was a certainty no unprejudiced jury could ever be gathered in that county. If Dinsmore had murdered ten men the same night, he would have secured a hung jury on the whole butchery.

That editor was a pretty slick writer, when you come right down to it. He made Dinsmore out the most dashing young hero that ever galloped out of the pages of a book. It was almost a book that he wrote about him!

He declared that if Dinsmore were anything worse than an impulsive youngster who didn't know better, he, the editor, would confess that his editorial brain was not worth a damn, and that he had never been able to judge a man.

Of course, the chief point in the interview was Dinsmore's own account of his fight with me. That was the main matter, all the way through. Because Dinsmore had called at the editor's office in order to explain to the world why he did not ride back into the mountains in order to answer my challenge.

I won't put in any of the bunk with which that article was filled, where the editor kept exclaiming at Dinsmore and asking him how he dared to venture through the streets unmasked—and how he had been able to scale the sheer side of the building.

I leave out all of that stuff. I leave out, too, all that the editor had to say about Dinsmore's family—how old that family was—how rich the estate was—how good and grand and gentle and refined and soldierly and judgelike the father of Dinsmore had been. How beautiful, womanly, gentle, and Southern his mother had been. How Dinsmore himself seemed to combine in himself all of the good qualities of both of his parents.

"So that," said the editor, "I could not help feeling that what this young man was suffering from was an overplus of talents, of wealth, of social background. His hands had been filled so completely full since his childhood with all that other men hunger for, that it was no wonder he had turned aside from the ordinary courses of ordinary men. Alas, that he did not live in some more violent, more chivalric age! Then his sword and his shield would have won a name."

The editor rambled on like this for quite a spell. Not very good stuff, but good enough to do for a newspaper. Newsprint stuff has to be a bit raw and edgy in order to cut through the skin of the man who reads as he runs.

The whole sum of it was that Jeffrey Dinsmore was a hero, and that he was a little too good for this world of ours to appreciate.

Finally, Dinsmore told about me.

He had gone up into the mountains, to Elmira, he said, because he wanted to find me where I would be at home among my own friends—because he didn't want to take me at a disadvantage.

"But why did you go in the first place?" asked the editor.

"I'm rather ashamed to confess it," said Dinsmore, with an apologetic smile, "but when I heard of all of the atrocities of this fellow Porfilo, and how he had butchered men—not in fair fight but rather because he loved butchery—and how helpless the law had proved against him—well, sir, I decided that I couldn't stand it, and so I decided that I should have to get up into those mountains, and there I'd meet Mr. Porfilo hand to hand and kill him if I could!"

The editor couldn't let Dinsmore say any more than this without breaking in to comment and praise Dinsmore and show that he was like some knight out of the Middle Ages riding through the dark and unknown mountains to find the dragon.

Well, as I said before, that editor was a good editor, but what he had to say began to get under my skin. I looked again at his picture. He had a thin face and he wore glasses.

I wonder why it is that spectacles always make me pity a man?

Dinsmore went on to tell how he had met me, and how I had whirled on him and fired the first shot, while he was waiting to talk. Well, that was all very true. Twenty people could swear to the truth of that, but not one of them had the sense to know that I had fired wide.

Then he said that the firing of that first shot showed him that I was a coward and a bully—a coward because I was a bully, and a bully because I was so very willing to take advantage of another man who only wanted to stand up and fight fair and square.

I couldn't read farther in the paper at that time. I had to walk up and down for a time to cool off. Then I looked hurriedly through the paper to try to find a statement by Dick Lawton, or somebody like that, defending me. But there wasn't any such statement. Only, on the fourth and fifth pages of the paper there were opposite accounts of the pair of us.

On one page there was the story of Dinsmore, with little illustrations inset, showing the great big house that he had been born and raised in; and how Dinsmore looked in his rowing squad at college in the East, and how Dinsmore looked in his year of captaincy of the football team, when his quarterback run had smashed the Orange to smithereens in the last two seconds of the game.

It showed how he looked on a polo pony—and what the five girls looked like that he had been engaged to at various times in his life—and how he looked standing beside his father, Senator Dinsmore—and how he looked arm in arm with his dear old mother—and how he looked when he rode the famous hunter, Tippety Splatchet, to victory in the Yarrum Cup.

Well, there was a lot of stuff like that, with the history of his life written alongside of it.

On the opposite page it showed the house I was born in in Mendez, and there was a picture of the butcher shop that my father had owned. There was a picture of myself, too, showing my broad face and heavy jaw and cheekbones.

"Like a prizefighter of the more brutal kind!" Dinsmore had said.

But there was only a dull account of my affairs—"butcheries," the editor called them. I was made out pretty black, and there was not a word of truth said to defend me. When I got through, I wanted to kill that editor!

I went back to Dinsmore's account. He told how he had decided that I was a swine, and then he had fired after my second shot, and the bullet had wounded me in the head—after which I spurred the mule away down the street as fast as I could!

There were plenty of witnesses who could prove that the bullet stunned me and that I did not begin to flee of my own free will. But of course none of their statements was wanted. Nothing but the word of the hero!

As for coming back into the mountains, Mr. Dinsmore said that after standing in the street of Elmira and firing shot after shot "into the air" and watching me ride "like mad" to get away from danger, he had no wish to come back to find me again.

He said that he felt he had fairly well demonstrated that the bully Porfilo was a coward at heart. He, Dinsmore, feared a coward more than he did any brave man. For a coward was capable of sinking to the lowest devices! He knew quite well that if he accepted the invitation to face the challenge of Leon Porfilo, he would be waylaid and murdered!

So much for his opinion of Leon Porfilo.

Now, as I read this letter, such a madness came over me that I trembled like a frightened girl. Then I steadied myself and sat with my head in my hands for a long time, thinking, wondering.

But what I made out at last was rather startling.

For it was declared in the paper that Mr. Dinsmore had said that he was in the capital city because he was then engaged in the task of drifting himself rapidly East and that the West perhaps would see him never again.

But, as I read this statement, I could not help remembering that I had seen him once before in the capital city, and I remembered, also, all of the nasty thoughts that had gone through my mind at that time.

## · · · 22 · · ·

Perhaps I should hardly call them "thoughts," when they were really no more than premonitions, based upon the prettiness of the governor's wife and the thoughtfulness of the governor—and Jeffrey Dinsmore, gentleman and gunman, climbing the back fence of the governor's house at full speed.

I considered all of those things, and the more that I thought of them, the more convinced was I that the celebrated Dinsmore was *not* passing through the capital city—certainly not until he had seen beautiful young Mrs. Shay.

So I turned the matter back and forth in my mind for three whole days, because I am not one of those who can make hair-trigger decisions and follow them. The result of all of my debating was that I saddled Roanoke and began to work some of his fat off by shooting him eastward.

We came through the upper mountains, and I had

my second view of the lowlands beneath me, silvered and beautified in evening mist. Once more I reached the lowest fringing of trees in the foothills and slept through a day. Once more I started with the dusk and drove away toward the city. Not the city, now! But in my mind there were in it only three people: William P. Shay, his wife, and Jeffrey Dinsmore.

Naturally I passed that last name over my tongue more frequently than I did the other two. Every time it left the acid taste of hate. I was hungry—hungry to get at him. Not that I feared him less than I had been fearing him. Simply that my hatred was too intense a driving force to let me stay away from him.

On the second night I was on the edge of the town, as before, and in the very same hollow where I had left Roanoke before, I left him this time. Only that I did not keep a saddle on him because I was hardly capable of doing all of my work in a single evening in the town.

I hid the saddle in the crotch of a lofty tree, and with the saddle I left my rifle and all my trappings except a little stale pone, hard almost as iron, but the easiest and most compact form, almost, in which a person can transport nutriment. I tucked that stony bread into my pockets. I had two heavy Colts and a sheath knife stowed handy in my clothes. Then I was ready to take my chances in the city again.

I walked in by the same route, too, except that when I came through the deserted outskirts of the city I began to bear away to the right, because I had a fairly accurate idea of where the governor's house was located. As a matter of fact, I brought up only two blocks away from it, and presently I came in behind that house.

I had made up my mind before, and I put my determination into action at once. The house was fenced, behind, with nine feet of boards as I have said before. But I managed to grip my hands on the upper edge and swing my body well over them by the first effort. I dropped close to the ground and squatted bunched there to look over the lay of the land and see what might be stirring near me.

There was not a soul. The screen door of the back porch slammed and I heard someone run down the steps. However, whoever it was kept on around the house by the narrow cement walk. I heard the heels of that man click away to dimness; I heard the rattle of the old front gate, and then I started for the corner stables.

Once that barn had been much bigger. One could tell by the chopped-off shoulders of the barn that it had once extended wide, but now perhaps it was the carriage shed which was trimmed away, and the barn that remained stood stiff and tall and prim as a village church.

I didn't care for that. I slipped through the open door of it and stood in the dark, smelling and listening —smelling for hay and finding the sweetness of it—and listening for the breathing of horse or cow—and not hearing a whisper!

So I went a little farther in and lighted a match. It was exactly as I had prayed. There was a heap of very old hay in one end of the mow—perhaps it had been there for years, untouched. The dry, dusty floor of the horse stalls showed me that they had not been occupied for an equally long time. This was what I wanted. I decided that people would not readily look for Leon Porfilo in the governor's barn—no matter how imaginative they might be!

I was a little tired, so I curled up in that haymow and slept until a frightened mouse squeaked, half an inch from my ear. Then I sat up and snorted the dust out of my nose and nearly choked myself to keep from sneezing. When I passed out into the night, I found that the lights were still burning in the Shay house.

There was an inquisitive spirit stirring in my bones that evening. The first thing I did was to remove my boots and my socks. I figured that my calloused feet would stand about all the wear that I would give them that night.

I left boots and socks in the barn. I left my coat with them. I took all the hard pone and the sheath knife and one revolver out of my clothes. Then I rolled up my trousers to the knees. By that time I was about as free as a man could wish, except he were absolutely naked. I felt free and easy and *right*. I could fight, now, or I could run. Also, I could investigate that tall old house. I guessed that there was enough in it to be worth investigation.

First I took a slant down to the window of the governor's little private room. I skirted around through the lilac bushes, first of all. When I had made sure that none of those infernal detectives were hanging about to make a background for me, I drew myself up on the window sill and surveyed the scene inside.

It was what I suspected. That was the governor's after-hours workshop—and I suppose that he spent more hours there than in his office. Here he was, with a secretary on one side taking shorthand notes, and beyond the door there was the purring of a typewriter where another secretary was pouring out copy of some sort. Governor Shay was just the same man in worried looks that I had known before.

I spent no time there. He was not the man I wanted. First I skirted around the house and peered into other rooms until I made out that Mrs. Shay was not in any of them. Then I climbed up to a lighted window in the second story. It was easy to get to it, because there was a little side porch holding up a roof just beneath it.

I curled up on that roof and looked inside. There I found what I wanted!

Yes, it was more than I could have asked for! There were all of my suspicions turned into a lightning flash before my eyes! There was Mrs. Shay, and, standing before her was that celebrated young man of good breeding, Jeffrey Dinsmore, doing his very best to kiss her.

But if he were masterful with men, he was not able to handle this slender girl. She did not speak loudly, of course. Her words hardly carried to me at the window. But what she said was:

"None of this, Jeffrey! Not a bit of it!"

He stepped back from her. I've seen a man step back like that when a hard punch has been planted under his heart. That was the way Jeffrey Dinsmore stepped away. The pain in his face went along with the rest of the picture. He was a badly confused young man, I should say. That was not what he had expected.

Mrs. Shay was angry, too. She didn't tremble; she didn't change color; she didn't change her voice, either. She wasn't like any girl I had ever seen before in that way. But one could feel the anger just oozing out of her, so to speak. Jeffrey began to bite his lip.

"I didn't think that you would use me quite so lightly," said she. "I didn't expect that!"

He said: "I am a perfect fool. But seeing you only once in weeks and long weeks—and thinking of you, and breathing of you like sweet fire all the time I am away—why, it went like flame into my brain, just now. I won't ask you to forgive me, though, until you've had a chance to try to understand."

He said it quietly, with his eyes fixed at her feet.

While he stood like that, I saw a flash of light in her eyes, and I saw a ghost of a smile look in and out at the corner of her mouth. I knew that she really loved him—or thought she did.

"I ought to have time to think, then," said she. "I'm afraid that I'll have to use it. I am just a little angry, Jeffrey. I don't want to spoil our few meetings with anger. It's a dusty thing and an unclean thing, don't you think so?"

He kept his head bowed, frowning, and saying nothing. This wasn't like my mental picture of him. I thought he would be all fire and passion and lots of eloquence—buckets full of it! Then I saw. He was taking another role. He was being terse and very plain—that being the way to impress her, he thought.

"So you'd better go," said she.

He answered: "I'll go outside—but I'll wait—in the hope that you'll change your mind."

"Good-by," said she.

I expected him to come for the window. Instead, he opened the door behind him and quickly stepped out into a hall!

I was down from the roof in a moment, and I began to rove around the house, waiting for him to appear. For five or ten minutes I waited. Then I realized that there must be more ways of getting in and out of that house than I had imagined. There might be half a dozen cellar exits and ways of getting from the second story to the cellar.

It was a time for fast thinking, and this time I was able to think fast, heaven be praised!

What I did was to swing up to the roof of the porch and get back to the window where I had witnessed this little drama. Mrs. Shay was lying on a couch on the farther side of the room, and her face was buried in a cushion. Her shoulders were quivering a little.

However, I had no pity for her, because I was remembering the face of the governor.

I simply slid through the window and stood up against the wall. The floor creaked a couple of times under my weight.

"Yes?" said she.

I suppose she thought that it was someone at the door, tapping.

"There is no one there," said I.

## • • • 23 • • •

Oh, she was game! She didn't jump and squeal, but she looked around slowly at me, fighting herself so hard, that when I saw her eyes they were as cool as could be. But when she managed to recognize me, she went white in a sickening way, and stood up from the couch and crowded back into the corner of the room. She said nothing, but she couldn't keep her eyes from flashing to the door.

I said: "I have that door covered, and I'll *keep* it covered. No help is coming to you. You're in here helpless, and you'll do what I tell you to do."

Still she was silent, setting her teeth hard.

I went on: "First of all, I'm going to wait here to make out whether or not Mr. Dinsmore was outside and saw me come through the window. If he saw me, I think that he's man enough to come after me."

There was a flash of something in her eyes. A sort

of assurance, I think, that it would be a bad moment for me when her hero showed up.

But still she wouldn't talk. Oh, she was loaded to the brim with courage. She was meeting me with her eyes all the time. I liked her for that. But that was not enough. There was something else for which I hated her. It was boiling in me.

I went on to explain: "When I saw him leave the room, I went down to the yard and tried to find him as he came out of the house. But he must have vanished into a mist."

At that the words came out quickly from her: "Were you watching when he left the room?"

"Yes," said I, and I looked down to the floor, because I didn't care to watch her embarrassment. But, for a moment, I could hear her breathing. It was not a comfortable moment, but sooner or later, I had to let her understand what I knew.

"If Mr. Dinsmore—" said she, and stopped there.

"If he doesn't come back," said I, "I don't know what I'll do—yes, I have an idea that might pass pretty well!"

So we waited there. That silence began to tell on her and it told on me, too, partly because I was waiting for Dinsmore's step or voice and partly that just being with that girl in that room was a strain.

It was not that she awed me because of the fact that she was the governor's wife, but just because she was a lady, and this was her room, and I had not a right in it! It was full of femininity, that room. It fairly breathed it. From the Japanese screen in the corner to a queer sort of a vase of blue stuck in front of a bit of gold sort of tapestry—if you know what I mean.

Well, I stood in the corner of that room, with the ceiling about an inch above my head, and as I stood there, I was conscious, I'll tell a man, that my feet and legs were bare to the knees from my rolled-up trousers—and I knew that my shirt was rolled up, too, to the elbows—and that my hat was off and that the wind had blown my hair to a heap—and that I was sun-blackened almost to the tint of an Indian.

I was a ruffian. I had a ruffian's reputation, and yonder was the governor's wife looking like the sort of a girl that painters have in their minds when they want to do something extra and knock your eye out.

No, I wasn't extra happy as I stood there, and neither was she. The pair of us were waiting for the sound of his feet.

Then she said: "Do you think that I'll keep silent when I hear him—if he comes?"

"You may do what you want," said I. "But if you make a sound, he won't be the only one that hears!"

No doubt about it, a gentleman couldn't have said such a thing. Well, a gentleman I cannot pretend to be!

I said: "You'll make no noise. You'll sit tight where you are."

So she looked quietly up to me and studied me with grave eyes. How cool she was! Yet I suppose that this situation was more terrible to her than a frowning battery of guns pointed in her direction.

"Do you imagine," said she at last, "that I shall permit you to murder him?"

I answered her quickly: "Do you imagine that I wish to murder him?"

Her eyes widened at me.

"I understand," said I. "Dinsmore has filled your mind with the same lies which he has published in other places. It is going to be my pleasure to show you that I am not a sneak and a coward, even if I have to bully you now—for a moment!"

Then she said: "I almost believe you!"

She looked me up and down, from my tousled head of hair and my broad, ugly, half-Indian features, to my naked toes gripping at the floor.

"Yes," said she, "I do believe you!"

It was a great deal to me. It almost filled my heart as much as that first moment when Mike O'Rourke said that she loved me.

"But if he has not seen you? If he is not coming?" said Mrs. Shay.

"Then you will make a signal and bring him here to me!"

She shook her head. "What would happen then?"

"You guess what will happen," said I. "I have no mercy for you. I have seen the governor. I think he is a good man and a kind man."

"He is," said she, and dropped her face suddenly into her hands.

"If you will not call Dinsmore back, I shall go to the governor."

"You will not!" gasped she, not looking up.

"I shall!"

Then she shook her head. "I have no right for the sake of my own reputation—or what—"

"Listen to me," said I, standing suddenly over her so that my shadow swallowed her, "if you speak of rights, have you a right to touch Governor Shay? This thing would kill him, I suppose."

She threw back her head and struck her hands together. Just that, and not a sound from her. But, I knew, that was her surrender.

Then she stood up and went to the window, and I saw her raise and lower the shade of the window twice. Then she returned to her place, very white, very sick, and leaned against the wall.

"I am sorry," said I.

But she made a movement of the hand, disclaiming all my apology.

"There will be a death," said she huskily. "No matter what else happens, I shall have caused a death."

"You will not," said I. "Because after two men such as Dinsmore and I have met, we could not exist without another meeting. Will you believe that, and that our second meeting must come and bring a death?"

She cast only one glance at me, and then I suppose that there was enough of the sinister in my appearance to give her the assurance that I meant what I said.

"Because," I went on, "one of us is a cur and a liar. I hope that heaven knows which one by the fight! You are going to be standing by!"

"I!"

"You are going to be standing by," I insisted.

She dropped her head once more with a little gasp, and so the heavy silence returned over us again. It held on through moment after moment. I thought that it would never end.

Perspiration began to roll down my forehead. When I looked to the girl, I could see that her whole body was trembling. So was mine, for that matter.

But, at last, no louder than the padding of a cat's foot, we heard something in the hall, and we did not have to ask. It was Dinsmore! As if he had been a great cat, I could not avoid dreading him. I wished myself suddenly a thousand miles from that place.

His tap was barely audible; and the voice of Mrs. Shay was not more than a whisper. The door opened quickly, and lightly. There was Dinsmore standing in the doorway with a face flushed and his eyes making lightnings of happiness until his glance slipped over the bowed figure of the girl and across to me in the corner, dressed like a sailor in a tropical storm.

Then he shut the door behind him as softly as he had opened it.

He stood looking from one of us to the other, and there was a fighting set to his handsome face, although the gaiety and the good humor did not go out of it for a moment. I felt, then, that he was invincible. Because I saw that he was a man unlike the rest of the world. He was a man who *loved* danger. It was the food which he ate, and the breath in his nostrils.

He only said: "I thought it was only a social call; I didn't know that there was work to be done. But I am very happy, either way!"

## ··· 24 ···

Even the sang-froid of this demidevil, however, could not last very long; for when his lady lifted her face, he saw enough in it to make him grave, and he said to me:

"You could not stand and fight, but you could stay to talk, Porfilo!"

Then I smiled on this man, for somehow that touch of malice and that lie before the girl gave me a power over him, I felt.

So I said to him: "We are going down to the garden, the three of us. The moon is up, now, and there will be plenty of light."

For the electricity in the room was not strong enough to turn the night black. It was all silvered over with moonshine.

"What's the trick, Porfilo?" said Jeffrey Dinsmore. "Are you going to take me down where you have confederates waiting? Am I to be shot in the back while I face you?"

"Jeffrey!" said his lady under her breath.

It made him jerk up his head.

"Do *you* believe this scoundrel?"

Her curiosity seemed even stronger than her fear; for she sat up on the couch and looked from me to Dinsmore and back again to me, weighing us, judging us as well as she was able.

"Every moment," said she, "I believe him more and more!"

"Will you go down to the garden with us?" said he. "Will you go down to watch the fight?"

"Leon Porfilo will make me go," said she.

"He and you," said Dinsmore, "seem to have reached a very perfect understanding of one another!"

"You will lead the way," said I.

"Are you commanding?" said he with a sudden snarl, and the devil jumped visibly into his face. So that there was a gasp from the girl.

"As for me," said I, "I had as soon kill you here as in the garden. I am only thinking of the governor's wife!"

He bit his lip, turned on his heel, and led the way out of the room. I saw at once what the secret of his goings and comings was. This was a dusty little private hallway—and it connected with what was, apparently, an unused stairway. Perhaps, at one time, this had been the servants' stairs and then had been blocked off in some alteration of the building.

At any rate, it led us winding down to the black heart of the cellar, where I laid a hand on the shoulder of Dinsmore and held him close in front of me with a revolver pressed into the small of his back.

"This is fair play, you murderer!" said he.

"Listen to me," said I. "I know you, Dinsmore. Do you think that your lies about me have *convinced* me?"

This was only a whisper from either of us, not loud enough to meet the ear of the girl.

We wound out of the cellar and stood suddenly behind the house. There was a very bright moon with a broad face, though not so keen as her light in the high mountains. Enough to see by, however. Enough to kill by.

"Now," said Dinsmore, turning quickly on me, "how is this thing to be done?"

I could see that his hand was trembling to get at his gun. He was killing me with his thoughts every instant.

He added: "How is this to be done, with a poor woman dragged in to watch me kill you!"

"I needed her," said I, "to make sure that you would fight like a gentleman. Also, I needed her to see that, when I kill you, I shall kill you in a fair fight. Otherwise she might have some illusion about it. She might think that her hero had died by treachery and trickery. Besides, I wanted her here because, as the time comes closer, she will have a better chance of seeing that you are a cur or a rat! The devil keeps boiling up in you continually. She has never seen that before."

"Will you step back among the shrubbery?" said he to her.

"If I go," said she, "I shall only be turning my back on something that I ought to see."

"You will see me dispose of a murderer, and that is all."

"If he were a murderer, he could have shot you in the back—and the people who heard the sound of the shot would have found you lying dead—in my room—at night. The governor's wife!"

"You remember *him,* now!" said Dinsmore, his voice shaken.

"I remember him, now," said she, "and I hope that

I shall always remember him a little—if not enough!"

He clapped his hand across his breast and bowed to her. "Madame," said he, "I see that you are cold."

"Are you spiteful, Jeffrey?"

"Spiteful?"

He stepped backward, after that, and he faced me with a convulsed face. I could see, now, why she had been shrinking farther and farther away from him. She was having deep glimpses of the truth about this gentleman of good breeding, and of an old family.

"Are you ready, Porfilo?" said he quietly.

"Ah, God have mercy—" I heard the girl whisper. But I saw that she did not turn her head away. No, not even then.

"Do you know the time?" said I.

"I do not," answered Dinsmore.

"Do you, Mrs. Shay?"

"It is nearly ten—it is almost the hour."

"I have heard the big town clock," said I. "At the first stroke, then, Dinsmore!"

"Good!" said he. "This ought to be in a play. At what distance, my friend?"

"Two steps—or twenty," said I. "You can measure the distance yourself."

"Jeffrey!" cried the poor lady. "It is not going to happen—you—"

"It means something one way or the other," said I. "It has to be decided. There is a witness needed."

Now, as I said this, I looked aside, and I saw, through the shadows of the trees and dimly outlined at the edge of the moonlight, the tall, strong figure of a man. I hardly know how I knew him; but suddenly I saw that it was the governor's self who stood there.

It made my heart jump, at first, but instantly I knew that he had not come on the moment. He had been there from the first—or at least for a space of time

great enough to have heard enough to explain the entire scene to him. Yet that did not make my nerves
the weaker.

After all, it was his right to know. I really thanked
heaven for it, and that he should realize, if I died in
this fight, it was partly for his sake as well as for my
own. Or, if the other fell, it was also for his sake as
well as for my own!

Then, crashing across my mind, came the clang of
the town bell, and I snatched at the revolver.

It caught in my clothes and only came out with a
great ripping noise. I saw the gun flash in the hand of
Dinsmore and heard its explosion half drown the
scream of Mrs. Shay.

But he missed! Almost for the first time in his life,
he missed. I saw the horror and the fear dart into his
face even before I fired.

He was shot fairly between the eyes, turned on his
heel as though to walk away, and fell dead upon his
face.

The shadow among the shrubs reached him and
jerked him upon his back. It was the governor. He did
not need to tell me what to do, for I had already
scooped up the fainting body of Mrs. Shay and carried it toward the house.

There, close to the wall, he took her from my arms.

"Ride, Porfilo!" he said. "I shall keep my promise.
God be with you!"

But I did not ride. I went back and stood beside the
body of the fallen man until the servants came tumbling out of the house and swarmed about me. I tried
to get one of them to come to me and take me a prisoner and accept my gun. But they were too afraid.
One of them had recognized my face and shouted my
name, and that kept the rest away.

At length, one of the secret-service men who were

presumed to keep a constant guard about the house of the governor, came to me and took my gun.

Then he marched me down the main street of the town to the jail. A crowd gathered. Perhaps it would have mobbed me, but it heard the great news that the brilliant Dinsmore, the great gunfighter, was dead, and that numbed them.

## · · · 25 · · ·

Well, when the doors of the jail closed behind me, and when I was hitched to irons in my cell, I decided that I had been a fool and that the wild life in the mountains had been better than such an end to it. But when Mike O'Rourke came up from the southland and looked at me through those bars, I changed my mind. After all, it was better to live or to die with clean hands.

I began to discover that I had friends, too. I discovered it partly by the number of the letters that poured in to me. I discovered it partly by the amount of money which was suddenly subscribed to my defense.

But I did not want a talented lawyer at a high price. What I felt was that the facts of my life, honestly and plainly written down, would be enough to save me and to free me. I wanted to trust to that. So I had Father McGuire, who had been my guardian up to the time that I broke jail and became an outlaw, and who was one of the first to appear, select a plain, middle-aged man.

He was staggered at the fine fee offered him. He was staggered also by the importance of this case which was being thrust into his hands. So he came to me and sat down in the cell with me and looked at me with mild, frightened eyes, like a good man at a devil.

He wanted to assure me that he knew this case would make him a fortune by the notoriety which it would give him. He wanted to assure me that his wife begged him with tears to accept the task. But he had come in person to assure me that he was afraid his conscience would not let him take a case which, he was afraid—

I interrupted him there by asking him to hear my story. It took four hours for the telling, what with his notes, and his questions. Before the story was five minutes old, he said that he needed a shorthand reporter. There was no question about him wanting the case after that!

He took down that entire report of my life, from my own lips. A very detailed report. I talked for those four hours as fast as I could and turned out words by the thousand. When it was all ended, he said: "I only wish to heaven that I could make people see the truth of this, as you have told it to me! But seven years have built up a frightful prejudice!"

"Give it to the newspapers," I told him.

He was staggered by that, at first. To give away his case into the hands of the prosecution? But I told him that I would swear to every separate fact in that statement. So, finally, he did what I wanted, and against his will.

I suppose you have seen that statement, or at least heard of it. The editor of the local paper came to see me and begged me for a little intimate personal story to lead off with—an interview. I asked him if he were the man who wrote up the statement of Dinsmore.

He said that he was and apologized and told me that he realized since I had beaten and killed Dinsmore in a fair fight, that there was nothing in what Dinsmore had said. He begged me to give him a chance at writing a refutation. Well, I simply told him at once that he did not need to ask twice. He was the right man in the right place, and I told him to do his editorial best, to give me journalistic justice.

He did! He began with the beginning and he finished with the end. He made me into a hero, a giant, almost a saint. I laughed until there were tears in my eyes when I read that story. Mike O'Rourke came and cried over it in real earnest and vowed that it was only the truth about me.

However, that editor was a great man, in his own way. He didn't really lie. He simply put little margins of embroidery around the truth. Although sometimes the margins were so deep that no one could see the whole cloth in the center!

That great write-up he gave me saved my skin, at the trial.

But while the trial was half finished, another bolt fell from the blue when the governor announced that, no matter what the jury did, he intended to give me a pardon after the trial was over.

From that point I had the governor's weight of authority so heavily telling in my favor that the trial became a sort of triumphal procession for me. There was no real struggle, for public opinion had begun to heroize me in the most foolish way in the world. I was still a prisoner when people began to ask for autographs.

You know how it goes when the newspapers once decide to let a man live. The jury itself would probably have been lynched if it had so much as decided to divide on my case. They were only out for five minutes.

When they brought in a verdict of acquittal, the real joke about that matter was that they were right and not simply sentimental, because as I think you people will agree who have followed my history down to this point, I had not as yet committed a real crime. The cards had simply been stacked against me.

Three great factors fought in my behalf—the governor's word first—the honesty of my stupid lawyer—and the genius of that crooked editor! I don't know which was the more important. But what affected me more than the acquittal, was the face of Mike O'Rourke in the crowd which cheered the verdict.

# Sea Change

# Sea Change

## Diane Tullson

orca soundings

ORCA BOOK PUBLISHERS

**Library and Archives Canada Cataloguing in Publication**

Tullson, Diane, 1958-
Sea change / written by Diane Tullson.
(Orca soundings)

Issued also in an electronic format.
ISBN 978-1-55469-333-7 (bound).--ISBN 978-1-55469-332-0 (pbk.)

I. Title. II. Series: Orca soundings
PS8589.U6055S42 2010        jC813'.6        C2010-903617-4

First published in the United States, 2010
**Library of Congress Control Number:** 2010929069

**Summary:** Lucas rarely sees his father. On a trip to reconnect on the remote north
coast, Lucas discovers that kinship goes beyond blood, and that while he can't pick
his relatives, he can find his own community.

**Mixed Sources**

Cert no. SW-COC-001271
© 1996 FSC

FSC

*Orca Book Publishers is dedicated to preserving the environment and has printed
this book on paper certified by the Forest Stewardship Council.*

Orca Book Publishers gratefully acknowledges the support for its publishing
programs provided by the following agencies: the Government of Canada
through the Canada Book Fund and the Canada Council for the Arts,
and the Province of British Columbia through the BC Arts Council
and the Book Publishing Tax Credit.

Cover design by Teresa Bubela
Cover photography by Getty Images

ORCA BOOK PUBLISHERS
PO Box 5626, Stn. B
Victoria, BC Canada
V8R 6S4

ORCA BOOK PUBLISHERS
PO Box 468
Custer, WA USA
98240-0468

www.orcabook.com
Printed and bound in Canada.

13 12 11 10 • 4 3 2 1

*To Stan and Dorota, with love*

# Chapter One

I adjust my headset over my ears, and the noise of the helicopter drops to a dull thud. I feel the noise as much as hear it, as if the helicopter is a drum and I'm inside it. My seat faces out—the penalty box, the pilot called it—and the door is right in front of my knees. The window in the door has instructions about how to push it out in an emergency.

And about how not to open the door in flight, as if anyone would do that. Still, I pull my knees back from the door lever.

My father is sitting up with the pilot. He's got a communications headset and he's chatting with the pilot, laughing about something. His hair used to be darker than mine, more of a sandy brown, but now it's got some gray. He has deep lines around his eyes. Basically, he looks old.

Through the window, below, acres of trees roll out in all directions. That's all I've seen since we left the airfield in Sandspit—trees. Sometimes a stream ropes through the trees, but there's nothing else, no roads, no cut-lines. The pilot said a crew was logging on the other side of the ridge, but here I might be the first guy to see this forest. Well, me and the pilot. And my old man.

God, it is cold. The last of a nasty flu bug gnaws my gut. It got me a week off school though. Half the school has it, and apparently it's policy of the cook training program to make sure I don't infect the other half. My mother didn't give me too much grief about going. It's about time you spent some time with your father, she said. He had a flu shot, so he isn't going to catch it.

Except for us, the helicopter is empty. The tourist season finished a month ago. We're going to fish late-running salmon—coho, not that I'd know a coho from any other kind of fish.

My dad has been at the fishing lodge his entire working life, practically owns the place now. I'm seventeen and this is the first time I've been up. People pay plenty to fish the best salmon on the Pacific Northwest, he says. Only room for paying guests, he says. We'll go in October, after shutdown, he says.

We almost went fishing three years ago, but the weather turned bad and grounded the helicopter. That was the year Mom and I moved to Torrance. Between school and Dad's schedule, I haven't seen him since. Not that I saw much of him before the divorce—he spends half the year at the lodge and the other half on the road doing sportsman's shows. Maybe he's always looked this old and I just haven't noticed.

This year he was in LA, on business, and he called me up. I had the week off school and no good reason to say no. Dad said the coho are huge this year, and I want a big fish, a monster. I want a fish so big the old man pays to get it stuffed and hangs it in the lodge with a brass plate with my name on it.

Endless trees. There's nothing to mark this place. I could be anywhere.

The helicopter lifts over a rise and now I can see the inlet. The trees have been cleared near the water, and there are buildings—the fishing lodge. The docks are pulled up for the winter and look like gray tiles at the edge of the water. A couple of boats bob on moorings. The pilot heads toward a grass strip between the shore and the buildings.

I see deer right where the helicopter is going to land, about seven of them, their heads down, grazing on the grass. They must be deaf—they're not moving and the helicopter is almost right over them. We're still high off the ground, but the downdraft flattens the grass.

One deer drops to its knees, then collapses. It shudders and then lies still. It looks dead, but I don't know how that could be. We couldn't have hit it—we're too high. The other deer lift their heads, and then, finally, they run off.

The helicopter lands but the pilot doesn't shut it down. He motions with his hand for me to wait. From in front of the main building, a lodge worker jogs toward the helicopter. With the coveralls,

I don't notice at first it's a woman, but up close I see she's young, about my age. She's wearing a headset over a cap, on backward, dark brown hair sticking out from under it, and yellow safety glasses. She opens my door and points at my headset. I take it off and leave it on the seat. The noise is huge. I get out and grab my bag. I'm taller than the girl, and she taps my arm and points up—the rotor. I duck my head.

Dad is already out, tossing duffel bags and boxes from the storage compartment in the tail of the helicopter. He secures the door and waves for me to get out of the way. The helicopter lifts and veers up the inlet, the noise of the engine echoing off the steep slopes, then disappears and leaves us in silence.

The girl in coveralls shoulders a duffel bag from the pile of stuff on the grass. Dad strides over to her—he's not smiling now.

"You do that again, Sumi, and I'll fire your ass." He stabs his thumb at the dead deer. "Get that thing out of here."

The deer's eyes are open and it still has grass in its mouth. There's a round black hole just behind its shoulder, a bullet hole, and there's blood on the grass. It has pronged antlers but it's not a big animal.

Sumi shrugs. She tosses the duffel bag to me and then heads to the lodge. I glance at my dad but he's got his back to me, his hands on his hips, looking out at the water. So I follow Sumi.

The lodge windows are boarded up for the winter and the entrance is sheeted in heavy plastic. It doesn't look like we're staying in the lodge.

"Where should I put our stuff?"

She gives me a long look, up and down, like she's assessing me. I'm wearing shoes I've had for a year and a rain jacket I bought when I still lived in Vancouver. I'm suddenly aware I need a haircut. She grabs a wheelbarrow leaning against the porch. I wait for her to answer, but she doesn't. She goes back to the dead deer and hauls it into the wheelbarrow in a smear of blood. Its hooves bounce over the side as she wheels it behind the buildings.

That went well.

I dump my bags on the porch and go to the pile from the helicopter. I grab a couple of boxes of what I hope is fishing gear and head down to the water. Dad has put on rubber boots, and he's loading an inflatable boat pulled up close on the stony beach. I hand him the boxes.

"So, those coho hungry?"

Dad looks at me, then at the sky. "Too late to go fishing now, Lucas."

It's maybe three in the afternoon. We left LA early in order to catch the flight from Vancouver to Sandspit.

I say, "We're not going fishing?"

He rubs his hair. I hate it when he does that. When he tries to get out of something, he always rubs his hair. "I'll be back tonight or first thing tomorrow. We'll go fishing then. We'll spend the whole day."

"Tomorrow! What am I supposed to do until tomorrow?"

He unties the boat and pushes it off the beach, stepping in as it floats clear. "You still do that whiny thing with your voice."

Whiny thing? "You're going to see her." I'm so mad I don't care what my voice sounds like. "You're going to see Deirdre."

His mouth tightens. "Tomorrow, Lucas. I promise."

Deirdre is the reason for the divorce. "What does that mean exactly—you promise?"

He starts the engine and gives it some gas. He waves, like he hasn't heard me. He motors over to one of the aluminum open fishing boats moored in the bay. He transfers the stuff, ties the inflatable to the mooring buoy and starts the engine on the fishing boat.

I do not believe this.

The fishing boat backs off the mooring and then powers up. White water curls off the front of the boat. It gets smaller and farther away.

I sit down on the stony beach.

Actually, I do believe this.

I watch until I can't see the boat anymore. I throw about nine hundred rocks in the water but he still doesn't come back, so finally I head up to the lodge.

# Chapter Two

My duffel bag is gone. I figure Sumi moved it. On the porch of one of the small out-cabins I see a pair of boots and a rifle leaning against the wall. It must be Sumi's cabin. There's no answer when I knock, so I push open the door. I see my duffel bag, and I go in.

The cabin is just one room with a woodburning stove in the middle.

The stove gives off some heat. A set of metal bunk beds fills one corner, and there's a small square table that's pretty nice and looks like it might have come out of the lodge. The chairs don't match the table. Hanging next to the table is a small framed painting of a girl dancing on a shore with whales in the background. I don't know anything about art but it's a pretty girl.

A stack of cardboard boxes lines one wall. Inside the boxes I see cans of coffee, soup, beans, tetra packs of milk and juice, bags of rice and spaghetti, a huge tub of Golden Crisco. In a big tin box I find two loaves of Wonder bread.

My stomach rumbles, a good sign. I haven't had an appetite in days. I spot a can of tuna and peel back the lid. There's no fridge that I can see, so I don't bother looking for mayo. I tip half the tuna onto a piece of bread and squish the bread into a torpedo. Some of the tuna plops out of one end of the bread and falls on the floor. I bite into the sandwich. It's good, amazingly good.

My mouth is still full and I'm making another sandwich when I hear footsteps on the porch. The door swings open and Sumi is standing in her socks, holding a plastic pail. She takes off her heavy rain jacket and hangs it on a hook by the door. The sleeves of the jacket are rolled up, like it's too big for her. She's still wearing the cap, but without the safety glasses she looks way more like a girl—a nice-looking girl.

She takes in my sandwich, the empty tuna can, my shoes and the spilled tuna. I try hard to swallow the lump of sandwich. She steps around me and sets the pail on the table.

I shouldn't have looked. The bottom of the pail is filled with a smooth red liver.

"Is that from the deer?"

She looks at me like I'm an idiot. "Where else would I get it?"

I can't help but think of a female Hannibal Lecter.

She opens the wood stove and jams in some sticks of wood. She blows on the embers and the wood catches. The fire crackles, and she adds a couple of split logs and then closes the door. On top of the stove she puts a heavy skillet.

"We're going to eat it?"

Another look. Sumi reaches into the bucket and grabs the liver. It slumps over her hand. She plops it onto a plate and pulls a knife from her side pocket. Holding the liver with one hand, she slices it into quivering pieces. The bite of sandwich I've only just managed to swallow threatens to come back up.

I say, "I'm actually not that hungry."

She looks at me, then at the empty tuna can. "I guess not." She pries the lid from the Crisco and uses a fork to gather a big blob. The tines of the fork leave marks in the yellow fat. The whole tub has fork marks. She flicks the fat into the hot pan and it starts to sizzle. From a big plastic jar she cups a handful of flour and coats the slices of liver. She drops the liver into the pan and then grabs a rag and wipes her hands. There's no sink and no running water, just a plastic dishpan. Maybe this counts as washing her hands.

Sumi rummages in one of the cardboard boxes and comes back to the stove with an onion. Using the same knife, she peels the onion in one big piece and then cuts it into rough chunks right in her hand. She puts the onion in with the liver and then plunks down in a chair.

I say, "So, this is your cabin?"

"I use it. In the winter I take care of the place." She has nice eyes, almond-shaped and golden brown.

"You don't go to school?"

"I'm done, graduated in June."

So she's older. But maybe not that much older. I turn eighteen in a couple of months. Maybe we're less than a year apart.

She says, "Your dad take off?"

Her question brings me back and I nod. "He had to see someone."

"That would be Deirdre." She smiles like she knows something. "She's my aunt. She and her kids live with my grandmother and me."

I feel like I've been transplanted into my father's other life. I look at Sumi, trying to imagine what her aunt looks like. I say, "Your grandmother's place, is it far?"

"No, a couple of hours."

"That seems far to me. He said he might not be back until tomorrow."

Sumi grins. "He won't be." Her front teeth look very white. "He usually brings her here. Maybe he's staying at our place because of you." She gets up and turns the meat in the pan.

Nice, having this time together, me and Dad—except that he's two hours away with his girlfriend.

It's already getting dark, and Sumi lights a Coleman lantern. She says, "He won't be on the water in the dark, not with the weather changing."

"Maybe we should phone him." Maybe, if he leaves right now, he can make it back and we can forget, again, why he left.

"No satellite phone in the off-season." Sumi shakes the pan and hot fat spits onto the stove. "And we're out of radio range."

There's no cell service either. My mom used to say it was convenient for Dad that she couldn't reach him.

"Anyway, he knows to check the weather." Sumi tips the liver and onions onto the same plate she used to prepare it. She forks a piece into her mouth and shoves the plate toward me. The liver is nicely browned and crusty. It actually smells pretty good. Still, I wave it away. Sumi seems glad. She digs in like she hasn't eaten for days.

I let her eat for a while, then make an attempt at conversation. "My dad seemed pretty pissed about you killing the deer."

Sumi shrugs.

"You sniped it, really. Assassinated it."

She stops chewing, looks at me, picks a hunk out of her teeth and starts chewing again. She says, "It died happy."

I snort.

Now her eyebrows lift. "I guess you don't hunt."

"I guess I don't."

"The deer, they're so used to the helicopters they don't even move.

When the helicopter is close like that, the deer can't hear anything."

She swallows, takes another bite. "Up here the deer are small but the bears are big, the biggest black bears you'll find. We see bears around the lodge sometimes, and usually they just wander through. This one time, though, the helicopter was coming in, full of guests, and the deer were out on the grass like always, and this bear showed up at the edge of the clearing. He waited until the chopper got close, and then he ran out and bagged a deer. The other deer didn't even know what happened. The bear dragged the deer into the woods and was eating it by the time we got the guests unloaded."

"That would be something to see."

She nods. "All the guests saw. One of them thought it was harsh, said we were endangering the deer." She laughs. "She thought we should kill the bear, like it was a murderer." She jams the last piece of liver into her mouth. "Or should I say an assassin?"

I say, "Okay, it was hunting for food. I get it."

"It must have been watching the deer for a while to figure out the whole helicopter thing. They do that, bears. Sit and watch you. You won't even know they're there." Sumi slides her plate into the frying pan, pours water in from a blue jerry can and covers the pan with a lid. She points to the top bunk. "You sleep there. Shitter's out back. Don't wake me up in the night."

"Whoa, you're sleeping here too?" I know it's a stupid question, but I can't believe she'd stay in the same cabin as a guy.

She says, "I've got a tent if you don't want to sleep in here. I use it when Denny's here."

"It's a nice tent," Sumi says, and then she looks at me. "I'm sure the bear is long gone."

Bear? "No, I mean, if it's okay with you, then I'm fine sleeping together." My face gets red hot. "In the same cabin."

She waves her hand as if to erase my stupid comment. "Whatever," she says, and she turns toward her bunk.

So much for happy hour. I go outside but it is dark, pitch-black dark. Water and land and trees all look the same: pitch-black dark. There's no way I'm going looking for a shitter, not with a big bear around. I shiver. Inside, in the light of the lantern, I can see Sumi cleaning her teeth into the dishpan. Nice. I step off the porch and piss on the grass. Then I wait for a while, long enough that she might think I went to the outhouse, and then I go back in. She's already in bed.

I avoid looking at her as I climb into my bed. The sleeping bag feels a bit damp but it's warm. "Sumi?"

She grunts.

"So, my dad keeps the deer here for the guests? Like an attraction or something?"

I hear her roll over, and then she snuffs the lantern. "It's not like there's a fence. He plants grass. The deer eat the grass."

"So the deer don't belong to him?"

"I didn't say that."

"So they do belong to him?"

She lets out a huge sigh.

I know I should let it go, but I say, "He thinks they belong to him?"

There's a long pause, and then she says, "If you haven't figured out your father by now, Lucas, I'm not sure why you're trying."

"My grandmother might like a rabbit or something in the meantime."

"I guess I knew that. Beef has to age too."

"At home we've got a shed for game. Hopefully Denny will get back, and then I'll be able to take it home today."

I try to keep my voice level. "You don't have to wait for him. You don't have to keep me company."

"Oh, I know that." She looks out to the bay. "I'm not going anywhere in a boat, not until it clears."

That probably means the old man isn't getting back either, which means I'm not going fishing.

She must see my expression because she says, "I wouldn't mind going fishing later."

She's throwing me a bone and I'm not too proud to take it. I can't help but grin.

Midmorning and Sumi's been gone a couple of hours. I've cleaned last night's frying pan and dishes, found my duffel bag and descummed myself, also found the outhouse, including a well-read stack of *Field and Stream*—what a surprise. My jacket isn't cutting it, so I put on Sumi's and unfold the sleeves. It fits pretty well, actually. In the pocket there's a cartridge. Must be for the rifle. I put it back in the pocket and head out to look around the grounds.

The wind has dropped and the rain too. At the edge of the forest, huge cedar trees drip rainwater. Seabirds drop and loop over the water. The guest cabins are nice. They cluster to one side of the main lodge, and each one looks out over the bay. Sumi's cabin and a few other buildings are behind the lodge. All the buildings except her cabin are shuttered for the winter, the doorways covered with poly. Farther back, pushed right out to the forest, is a slope-roofed metal building. It's boarded up too. There's a sign: *Generator*. Not that it's running, based on the total lack of electricity in Sumi's cabin. I wander around back and that's where I find the deer.

It's hanging upside down, by its back-legs, from a chain block and tackle on a log frame. It hasn't been skinned. I reach up and touch the fur along its neck. It feels smooth. Close like this, I can see a subtle pattern in the deer hair. When I touch it, the body rotates, the chain clunk-clunking in the block. Now I'm looking at the underside, and the body cavity is propped open with sticks and is totally empty, as if it was scraped clean. The deer's eyes are open and follow me as the body turns one way, then the other. It's not very big. I think about Sumi's bear story. A bear could drag this thing away, no problem. I glance around. It could drag me away too.

The forest seems quiet all of a sudden. I feel hairs lift on the back of my neck. Something's watching me, I can feel it. I spin and scan the forest. Nothing is moving. Nothing is making a sound. It's like there's no air.

How fast can a bear run? I eyeball the distance to Sumi's cabin. Too far. A small outbuilding is closer.

I sense it more than hear it, a long exhaled breath. All I can think of is the bear.

I run. I don't know how long it takes to reach the outbuilding, but in those endless seconds I decide I'm going full bore through the door. It's not that easy. My shoulder actually bounces on the plastic over the door. I take my boots to it and make some holes. Then I start ripping it with my hands and find the door handle. It's not locked, thank goodness, but it opens out, damn it. I am totally crazed. I yank on the door, using it like a giant pry bar. The heavy vinyl finally gives and I dive through the door. Then I scramble to get the door closed. Nothing works anymore. My hands feel like I'm wearing ball gloves, but I manage to yank it closed.

There's no light. I rip air into my lungs. My hands are shaking, so I make them into fists and jam them in my armpits.

Outside, something thumps on the stairs.

Can bears open doors?

I crab walk away from the door so fast that my head crashes into something, and what feels like every fishing rod known to man rains down on top of me. Still, I scrabble backward, and I feel rods snapping.

Then the door opens. In the sudden light, I see Sumi. She looks at the shredded plastic around the door. She looks at me, sitting on my ass and so relieved that it is her and not a bear that I'm actually giggling. She starts to laugh too, until she sees the pile of broken fishing rods. Then she starts to swear, every word I know and even some I don't, repeating a few choice ones for good measure.

# Chapter Four

We're in the tackle room, apparently, and I've made a bit of a mess. Sumi shovels the worst of it off to the side of the room. Still swearing, she picks out a couple of rods that escaped damage and sets these by the door. From a rack she tosses me a set of overalls and a bright yellow floater jacket. Then she points to a line of rubber boots. "Think you can find some boots without totally trashing them too?" She grabs a pair of heavy wool socks from a bin and jams them in her pocket.

I guess we're going fishing. I think maybe I should clean up the rods, but she's leaving so I scramble to my feet, grab a pair of size-ten boots and follow her.

The fishing boat we're going to use is moored about a hundred yards from shore. The dinghy Dad used is bobbing on a mooring buoy where he left it, which is absolutely no good to us. We have to carry down a fiberglass rowboat from the boat shed. Sumi takes one side, I take the other. It's not a big boat, but it weighs a ton and I'm starting to sweat. "This thing have a motor?"

Sumi tips her head at the oars in the bottom of the boat. "It's got you."

This should be good—I've never rowed a boat.

We have to go back up to Sumi's cabin for our stuff, which doesn't seem like much, just some bottles of water, a few granola bars and a plastic box of fishing gear, which Sumi insists on carrying. The bread and peanut butter is starting to look good, but Sumi doesn't stop to eat, so neither do I. We load rods and gear into the rowboat. I take the middle bench, and Sumi pushes us off. She plunks down at the back of the boat and starts fiddling with the rods. I jam the oars into the locks and start rowing.

When I tell people what my old man does, that he's in charge of a fishing lodge, they figure I fish all the time. They ask me what the biggest fish I've caught is. They ask me what kind of rod I use, what kind of line, like I would know.

Sumi glances up from her work. "Where the hell are you going?"

I look over my shoulder and see that the fishing boat is way off to the left. I say, "What genius made it so you have to row backward?"

Sumi rolls her eyes.

I get the boat pointing where it needs to go, then pick a big rock on the shore and visually line it up. It should work. Keep the rock in line, keep the boat going where it's supposed to.

Sumi doesn't even look up. "You're pulling left."

I concentrate on pulling evenly.

"Now right."

"It's the waves. They're throwing me off."

"These little things? These aren't waves."

The wind is cold, but the waterproof floater coat feels too warm.

We arrive at the fishing boat with a clunk, which makes Sumi mutter. She steps into the fishing boat, takes the rope from the front of the dinghy and ties it to the mooring buoy. Meanwhile, I'm still in the dinghy. It takes me a while to get back alongside the fishing boat, and with absolutely no grace I tumble into the bottom of the boat. Sumi sighs but doesn't say anything. She starts the big outboard and hollers at me to untie us. Then, before I can sit down, she guns the engine so I fall again, this time cracking my knees against the side of the boat.

"Hey," I shout. "I almost fell in!"

Sumi seems to smile. "One hand for the boat," she shouts back.

We motor out of the bay at what feels like full speed. Sumi stands and steers the outboard. She has pulled her hood up against the spray. I turn on my seat so the spray hits me in the back of my hood.

She's right. These aren't waves. They are watery brick walls. The boat slams into them and makes my teeth clack. Then the boat thuds into the trough, and each section of my spine jams together.

"How far are we going? Alaska?"

She doesn't answer but careens around a point of rock jutting into the sea. The rock is covered with sea birds. Some take wing as we blast by. It looks like the rock is painted white with bird crap.

Sumi throttles back. "Low tide. It's shallow in here." She picks her way through some invisible channel.

"How can you tell it's low tide?"

She gives me another you're-an-idiot look and points her thumb at the shore. A ragged row of logs and seaweed lines the beach far up from the water. "Twice a day up here we get high and low tides. And big enough that you know it—it's like the sea breathes in and out." She tamps the engine way back so we're barely moving.

It's quiet now. I can hear sea birds. Along the shore, massive cedar trees lean out from stony outcrops. Going this slow, Sumi doesn't have to steer the outboard all the time. Occasionally she reaches over and makes a small steering correction but otherwise her hands are free.

She grabs a fishing rod and pulls a bucket of small dead fish from under the other seat. She cuts the head off a fish and hollows out the body cavity, then flicks the head and guts into the sea. She weaves the fish hook into the bait, then drops the lead into the water. The headless fish looks like it is swimming.

"Cool," I say.

She shows me how to attach the line to a down rigger so that the bait stays at a certain depth. She rigs a second rod, plunks it into a rod holder and then settles back on her seat.

"Watch the tip of the rod. If it wiggles, you've got a bite."

"Like, wiggles how?"

"Like, it wiggles."

I stare at the end of the rod. Sumi sits with her hands in her pockets and her eyes half closed. I'm afraid to even blink in case I miss whatever it is I'm supposed to be watching for.

She says, "You've got one."

She's so calm I sit there for a moment wondering what she's talking about. Then I notice the end of the rod bending toward the water. I jump to my feet and grab the rod.

"Other way."

I glance down at the rod. The reel is on top. I feel my face flush, and I fumble the rod around so the reel is underneath.

"Set the hook."

She's calm. I'm not. "What does that mean, set the hook?"

She makes an upward yanking motion.
I do that.

"You've lost the fish," she says.

"No, I can feel something."

She shrugs. I reel in the line, waiting for the fish. Finally the hook pops to the surface. The bait is gone.

"I lost him."

She nods. "Didn't set the hook."

She makes me bait the hook this time. My headless fish looks less real. It flops more than swims.

Sumi says, "It probably doesn't matter."

"Like I won't be able to bring it in anyway? Oh, that's nice. It's not like I've been doing this all my life."

"Neither have I."

"You haven't always lived here?"

She shakes her head. "Lived in Vancouver with my mother. Moved up here three years ago."

"Your mom is from Vancouver?"

"She was from here. Left when she got pregnant and never came back."

"I guess she can fish."

"I guess not. She's dead."

"Oh." What do you say to that? "Sorry."

She doesn't seem to hear me. I don't even see the motion of her rod, but Sumi slips it from the holder. She holds it poised over the water.

"Do you have a bite?"

She ignores me. She lets out some line.

"Why aren't you setting the hook?"

She still doesn't answer. She rests her hand lightly on the line, as if she's listening with her fingers. After what seems a long moment, she snaps the rod upward and starts reeling. "Fish on!" she shouts. "Take the tiller!"

I grab the steering arm on the outboard. Good guess.

"Starboard!" she shouts as she reels. Starboard?

"Right! Go right!"

I pull the tiller to the right. We go left.

Sumi stumbles. "The other right!"

"Oh, like that makes sense." I push the tiller left and, sure enough, the boat turns right.

She's alternately reeling like crazy or letting line scream off the reel. I ask her why she's letting the fish run, and she answers, "Only way to catch him."

Like that makes sense either.

She says, "coho like to jump, and he'll fight right off the line. This tires him out, lets him get used to the idea of being caught."

A short distance off the boat, something silver flashes on the surface of the water. "Is that your fish?" It jumps and twists, throwing its head back and forth, trying to shake the hook.

She's reeling fast now. "Keep us heading straight."

I grip the tiller arm and the handle twists in my hand. The engine revs and we lurch forward. Oops. Sumi just about lands on her ass. She regains her footing and snarls, "Back off!" I twist the handle to throttle down on the engine and concentrate on steering.

She's got the fish close to the boat. It's frantic, flopping so its white belly flashes. I reach for the net, but in the time it takes to grab it from the front of the boat, Sumi has unhooked the fish and let it go.

"What the…?"

She says, "I always let the first one go."

"What if that's the only fish we catch?"

"Oh well." She watches as the fish recovers and swims away. Then she baits another hook and sends it down.

# Chapter Five

I manage to reel in a ten-pound coho. It won't break any records, but we take it because I'm not eating unknown deer parts for dinner and we're both so bloody cold we're just about ready to go in. At one point Sumi put on the wool socks she took from the tackle room. She was already wearing a pair of heavy socks. I've just got my regular socks and

I can barely feel my feet in the rubber boots, they're so cold.

"Fish on," she says, looking at my rod.

My hands fumble with the rod but I know what I'm doing now, more or less. I set the hook and start reeling. The rod end bends hard.

"It's big," she says.

It feels big.

She says, "Steady. Don't rip the hook out of its mouth."

I don't know where the fish is but it has a lot of my line. Despite the cold, I feel sweat prickle under my arms. I'm imagining this fish, a monster king, maybe forty pounds, bigger than anything my father has caught, maybe a record.

"Watch your line!"

The rod end tips down close to the boat. I pull it back up but it takes all my strength. Sumi gives the engine a shot of gas, and I'm able to reel in more line. It feels like I'm bringing up a refrigerator. Sumi's on her feet now, looking over the side of the boat.

"Holy crap."

"What?"

"It's a hali. A big one."

Still deep below the boat, I can see what looks like a massive green disc. "Halibut?"

"And on salmon tackle. She must not know she's hooked. Maybe you snagged her in the cheek."

My arms are threatening to snap. "How big?"

"Very big. Over a hundred pounds, easy. Don't let her see the boat. If she figures out what's going on she'll take everything you've got."

"She's got everything already. How do you know she's female?"

"A hali this size has to be female. Only the breeding females get this big."

I look at the net. "Uh, how do we get her into the boat?"

Sumi rummages in her tackle box and brings out a length of rope. Then she grabs a wooden pole with a nasty hooked end. "We'll use the gaff like a harpoon. We'll tie her to the side of the boat and let her bleed out. She has to be good and dead before we bring her in with us. I've heard of boats busted up by a thrashing hali." Sumi whistles and says, "She is one amazing fish." She stands with the gaff poised like a spear and says, "Ready?"

The halibut is almost motionless on the end of the line. It's like she's sleeping.

"How can she not know that she's hooked?"

Sumi says, "Hook is so light she doesn't feel it."

"So she's not going to fight?"

She laughs. "If she wanted off, you wouldn't be able to keep her on this light line. No one catches big fish like this, not without major halibut gear, and not without a hell of a lot of luck. Not many big halibut anymore, not here. My grandmother hasn't had a freezer full of halibut in years."

"So you've never caught a big halibut?"

She doesn't answer for a minute, and then she says, "I've kept some small ones."

My hands are starting to cramp. I say, "I've got a camera. Take a picture of it."

"Now?"

"It's in my pack. Get it and take a picture."

Sumi looks at me for a moment and then puts down the gaff. "You're letting her go."

I nod.

She digs out the camera and takes the picture. She takes another of me with the rod bent almost in two. I try to grin but I'm sure it looks more like a grimace. The halibut is taking every bit of strength just to hold it. I can only imagine what would happen if she fought.

Sumi takes out her knife. "Reel her in as close as you can."

It's stupid but I feel like crying. I'm exhausted and my feet are numb and I'm letting go the biggest fish ever.

Sumi leans down beside the boat and then looks up at me. "Are you sure?"

I'm not sure, not sure of anything. "Just do it."

Sumi smiles and cuts the line.

# Chapter Six

We've got enough wood in the stove that the metal sides glow red. I'm wrapped in my sleeping bag wearing everything I own, plus Sumi's jacket, and finally I've stopped shivering. Sumi hands me a mug of something hot, sweet and clearly alcoholic. I'm sure St. John's First Aid would be thrilled to know she's using alcohol to treat hypothermia.

Still, the drink leaves vapor trails of heat all through my gut and I feel ridiculously happy. Sumi pours the booze from a silver flask, tipping it over my mug to get the last drops.

I say, "So, no sign of my old man."

Sumi looks out the window at the sun, already low. "If he's not here by now, we won't see him today. He must be having a good time."

That should piss me off but I really don't care. Sumi turns to the stove and starts a pan for the salmon. I say, "At school we do this thing with salmon. It's like a crust of herbs. We wrap it in parchment and bake it over a pan of water."

Sumi digs out a blob of the ever-present Crisco. "Sounds like work." She moves the pan to the back of the stove and lays in a fat fillet of coho, skin side down. Then she grabs a bottle of maple syrup and douses the fish. She throws a lid on the pan and sits down across the table. "If you want rice or something, go ahead and cook it."

I get up but leave the sleeping bag wrapped around my shoulders. In the boxes at the side of the room I find a carton of rice and something way better.

"KD! I love KD!" So much for cook training. I grab two boxes of the mac and cheese. "It's a feast!"

Sumi shrugs, which I take as an enthusiastic yes, so I pour water into a pot and set it on the stove. "I'd like to be the guy who invented Kraft Dinner."

"You're a simple guy, Lucas."

Dinner is remarkably orange: salmon, KD and canned carrots. The salmon is amazing, clear-coated with an amber stickiness from the syrup. We both scarf down two plates, then mop up with a slice of bread. We sit back and groan.

"What's the biggest fish you've caught with a guest? Before today, that is."

She snorts. "You think you caught the biggest fish today?"

"I did. I know it."

She says, "I had a record coho jump right into my boat."

"You get a picture?"

"It jumped back out."

"You're full of it."

"No, that's the way it happened. Then another jumped in, and another. I had to put my arms over my head so I wouldn't get clobbered. It was like it was raining fish."

"Uh-huh."

"Then, right under my boat, the water turned black."

"Black."

"It was a whale, an orca. It surfaced right beside my boat. It blew and sprayed me with whale snot."

"I think we saw the same movie. Did it look at you with one wise whale eye?"

"It did! Then it dove and it had

these enormous tail flukes, it just about swamped me. But that's why the fish landed in my boat. They were trying to get away from the whale. No one caught another fish that day. They were all long gone because of the whale."

"So your guest, maybe he got a picture? Otherwise how can you prove you're not totally bullshitting me?"

"There wasn't a guest. I don't guide. Your dad says I'm no good with people."

"Well, you're not, actually."

She ignores that. "But that night, when I was tying up, the tide was coming in and I spotted something white at the edge of the water, snagged up in some kelp. I had to wade in and get it. It was a whale's tooth."

"Let me guess, it was the one from the killer whale. It gave you its tooth."

She grins. "That's right. It was the whale's way of saying sorry for scaring all the fish."

She's very pretty when she smiles. I say, "I didn't know whales lost their teeth. I thought it was sharks that could regrow their teeth."

"Well, it was a big tooth. It would have to be a big shark."

"Kind of like my dad. Maybe it was my dad's tooth."

She laughs. "Denny is harmless."

"No offence to your aunt or anything, but why haven't they got married?"

"Maybe they don't want to."

"Maybe he knows he can't commit."

"You're pissed because your parents got divorced," she says. "It happens. I don't know why you're not talking to him about it, Lucas." She chews her lip, as if she's thinking about what she wants to say. Finally she says, "There are way worse guys than your father."

I let that sink in while I wait for her to elaborate. But she doesn't. So I say,

"Okay, so you've got a whale's tooth. Is that why you always release the first fish you catch—for the whale? In return for the tooth?"

"No." She gets up. From the set of her shoulders I can see she's done talking. She says, "That's for my mother." She leaves and goes outside.

I drop the crusty plates into the dishpan and pour water over them, which I figure is a good start to cleaning up. Then I go out to the porch. The sun has almost dropped beneath the horizon. It's cold and feels like it could snow.

Sumi's rifle is leaning by the door. I go over and pick it up. The stock is some kind of wood, burnished like it's old. I put the rifle up to my shoulder and look down the sight. I imagine a deer, standing broadside, chewing grass. A tree becomes my imaginary deer. I take aim and squeeze the trigger.

*Click.* It's not loaded, of course.

I reach in my pocket for the cartridge I found earlier. In the dim light I'm not really sure what I'm doing, but I slip in the shell. I lift the rifle again and take aim at the tree.

Just then I hear Sumi's footsteps on the gravel path. I put the gun down and hope she doesn't see me with it.

If she does, she doesn't seem to care. She says, "What would be good right now is another drink."

# Chapter Seven

Why would I argue with her? "Might be some in the main lodge."

"You want to break into your father's fishing lodge and steal his booze?"

"We'll be careful. He won't ever know."

"Like the tackle room and how you were so careful with the fishing rods?"

She laughs. "He'll know. And anyway, there's no booze in there. They clear everything out at the end of the season."

"Maybe," I say.

It's dark now and I start across the grounds toward the main lodge.

"He won't be happy," she says, but she walks with me.

I don't really care how my father feels, but Sumi has to work with him, so I'm more careful with the plastic over the door than I was at the tackle room. I use Sumi's knife to pry out the staples holding the poly to the doorframe.

The lodge is dark and it feels colder than the air outside. Sumi pulls a small flashlight from her pocket. We're in a huge room. Tables and chairs are stacked against the windows. A great stone fireplace lines an entire wall. I spot the bar area, but the shelves behind the bar are bare. "Maybe the kitchen?"

"I doubt it," Sumi says.

She pads toward the back of the lodge, past a glass-walled office. My dad's name is stenciled on the glass by the door. I say, "He'll have some."

"No he won't. And anyway, it will be locked," she says.

I try the door and she's right. I peer in through the glass. Sumi hands me the flashlight, and I pan the light over the desk and bookshelves. Everything is tidy, but there's a mug on the bookshelf. I wonder if it's his coffee cup from the last day before shutdown and he left it there, the coffee congealed in the bottom of the cup.

My beam pauses on a series of picture frames on the bookshelf. My mouth goes a bit dry. I've stopped sending him a school photo. I've stopped going up to Vancouver at Christmas. I've stopped answering his emails. But no, these aren't my school photos. I don't recognize the people in the pictures. Each frame holds a shot of a guest with a big fish. Some are holding salmon, some are standing beside their fish hanging from the scale. There is a shot of a guy with a big hali—but not as big as the one we got today. Except for the coffee mug, there's nothing personal in my father's office. He could have my old school photo, at least.

"Come on," Sumi says.

The kitchen is long and narrow, smaller than the one at school but with nice prep tables. It's open to the dining area, and everything gleams in polished steel. I dive into the cabinets, rummaging in kettles and stock pots. Nothing has been left except a pail of dishwashing detergent. It's the same kind we use at school. From deep back on one shelf I see the gleam of glass.

"Bingo."

I emerge with a dusty almost-full bottle of something black. I pry off the lid and take a sniff.

"Fake Kahlúa. Yuck."

It's cold and thick but has the desired effect. I hand Sumi the bottle. She wrinkles her nose but takes a drink.

She slides down the cupboard to sit on the floor, holding out her hand so that I join her. She hands me the bottle. I'm not feeling so cold anymore. I take a drink. She takes a drink. I'm not a lightweight at parties, but this stuff goes right to my head.

Sumi reaches across and takes the flashlight from me. "We don't want to waste the batteries." She turns it off and the sudden blackness of the kitchen makes me gasp. She laughs. "Open your eyes."

"My eyes are wide open and I can't see a thing."

"Yes you can."

I feel her more than see her, like she's shifted so her face is in front of mine.

Do I imagine it, or can I smell maple syrup? If I leaned forward just a fraction, would I find her lips? Would she pull away? I say, "Sumi?"

I swear she is so close that I'm breathing her warm air. But she doesn't speak. I sense her moving away from me and I want to reach out and pull her back.

And then I can see her. It's like she breathed into the darkness and made it settle more lightly. I can see the outline of her hair and now the shape of her face. She's looking at me and I sense that she's smiling. I say, "Okay, yes, I can see."

She laughs and then rests her head on my shoulder. "You're more like your father than you know."

"My father?" I shudder. "That's a bit of a buzz kill."

She hands me the bottle. "Your dad doesn't touch this stuff."

I say, "No? Maybe it interacts badly with his male enhancement drugs."

She says, "Yesterday, when he lost it with me? He wasn't pissed about me killing the deer. He taught me how to shoot. My grandmother gave me the rifle. It's an old .303—used to be my grandfather's. She grew up in Japan and never learned to use a rifle. Anyway, the first time I tried, I managed to shoot a buck. But I nailed it in the flank. I was gone for two days tracking the deer before I could finally finish it."

I'm tempted to ask her how she got the deer out of the woods, that far away, but something tells me she didn't. And that it would bother Sumi, having to leave the deer.

She says, "So your dad, he showed me how to hit a deer clean in the lungs and heart."

"And you did. You got that deer with one shot."

"It helped that it was so close. I'm actually a terrible shot. Your dad knows that too."

I lean closer to her. Her hair smells good, like fresh air.

She says, "What he was pissed about was me shooting so close to the helicopter."

I sit up. "You mean you might have hit the helicopter?" I imagine the fiery carnage. "You could have killed us!"

She takes the bottle back from me. "And ruined a perfectly good helicopter."

"Jeez, Sumi, you have no idea how happy I am that you killed that deer."

She wipes her mouth with her sleeve. "He'll get over it. At least now my grandmother has meat for the winter."

"My dad might get over it. I'm not sure I will."

She gets to her feet and stretches. "Come on, let's get out of here while we still can."

I struggle to follow her, but it's dark, and on the way out I trip over a serving cart, which makes Sumi laugh really hard. At the front desk we snag a stapler and do a passable job resealing the poly around the front door. The staples are half the size of the ones we took out, but so long as no one gets too close, it looks like it did before.

The sky is clear and the moon hangs huge and yellow. There's barely anything left in the bottle. Sumi sways a bit, or else I'm swaying, it's tough to know. Then she stops still. "Listen," she says.

I don't hear anything at first. Then, faintly, I hear the clunk of a chain turning.

Sumi's eyes get big. "My deer!"

# Chapter Eight

"The bear's got my deer!" Sumi starts running toward the generator hut.

"Shouldn't we get your gun?"

She doesn't stop to answer, so I stumble across to her cabin and grab the gun. I can barely see her, but the moon lights the path. I feel the booze in my legs, but I'm not about to be left out here alone. I catch up with her.

I say, "What are you going to do if it's the bear?"

She's breathing hard. "First I'm going to take back my deer. Then I'm going to kick the bear's big butt. Then I'm going to run away just a bit faster than you." She holds her finger up to her mouth. "Quiet now."

"We're going to sneak up on it?"

She doesn't respond, just creeps toward the corner of the generator hut.

I'm beginning to question her judgement. Still, I follow her, my hands sweaty on the rifle. At the edge of the building she stops and motions for me to stay still. Then she tips her head around the corner. Quickly, she motions for me to join her.

The deer is swinging from the chain. So is the bear. The bear is clamped by its teeth onto the deer's antler. It would be funny except it's a very large bear.

Sumi bends to pick up a rock. Whooping, she jumps out and hurls the rock, nailing the bear in the ass. It grunts as if it is startled and drops to the ground. Sumi starts screaming and waving her hands, jumping up and down. The bear sits back on its haunches, looking at her.

"It doesn't seem too scared, Sumi."

"Jump up and down."

I jump up and down. Also I shout, scream and do something like jumping jacks.

The bear lowers its head. Then it gets onto its feet. Its head bobs back and forth as it sniffs the air. It's looking right at me.

Sumi throws another rock and I hear it thud on the bear's skull. It shakes its head and takes a step toward us.

My voice cracks. "Why don't you shoot it?"

She glances at me, then at the rifle. "Give me that thing." She swings the rifle up and aims it at the bear. I cover my ears and wait for the shot. But she doesn't shoot. Instead, she says, "*Bang.*"

Amazingly, the bear runs. There's the sound of crashing underbrush and he's gone. Sumi strides over and checks the deer. I'm keeping my eyes on the edge of the forest just in case the bear returns. My knees are actually shaking.

Sumi hefts the rifle over her head. "I am Sumi the Slayer!" She pumps the rifle in the air.

I duck out of the path of the gun. "Careful," I say.

She drops the rifle to her shoulder. "Like I'd let you run around the forest with a loaded gun." She aims the rifle at the ground, and it occurs to me she's going to fire it. She thinks it is unloaded because that's how she keeps the gun, but I'm thinking about the cartridge I loaded, and I can't get the words out in time. She squeezes the trigger.

# Chapter Nine

The blast of the rifle drives all noise from the forest. Then I hear Sumi scream. "My foot!" She collapses on the ground. "I've shot my foot!"

I think she could be joking, but then she leans over and throws up. The smell makes me blink, and I'm suddenly much more sober. I pick up the flashlight that she's dropped on the ground and shine it on her foot. It's hard to see but it looks like she stepped in something shiny. I bend and wipe a bit of it, then look at it under the flashlight. Blood. I drop to my knees and put the flashlight close to her foot.

She's screaming, and now I know it's for real. The side of her boot is torn open and a gush of blood pumps out onto the ground. Bits of her sock stick out of the wound. I see white things that I really hope aren't bone.

Sumi pants, "How bad is it?"

I lie. "Looks like your boot got most of it. There's some bleeding though. I'll take care of that."

I really did take a first-aid course. I had to in order to get into the cook training program. We learned how to wrap the end of a finger so it can be reattached.

Nothing is getting reattached on Sumi's foot. It looks like ground beef.

I take off the jacket and strip down to the cleanest thing I have—my shirt. I ball it up into a wad and press it onto the boot. Sumi swears and tries to pull her foot away. "Easy." I wrap the sleeves of the shirt around her boot, trying to contain most of her foot pieces. Blood soaks through the shirt. I tighten the sleeves so that there is more pressure over the wound.

"I need to get you back to the cabin."

Sumi is lying on her back now, her hands over her face. I think she's crying but she doesn't want me to see. There's no way she can walk. I look around and spot the wheelbarrow. It's been scrubbed clean. I get the wheelbarrow and bring it over.

"I'm going to help you up."

She nods and extends her hand. I haul her up, catching her arm around my shoulder. She hops on her good foot. Then she crumples into the wheelbarrow, holding her injured foot straight out.

The ground is rough and she curses at every bump we hit. But I manage to get her back to the cabin. She gets out of the wheelbarrow and sinks down face-first on the porch steps. I think she's going to be sick again, but she drags herself to the cabin door.

"Let me help you."

It's like I'm not even there. She drags herself in, half crawling, and heads straight for her bunk.

I light the lantern and spot a first-aid kit hanging by the door. Sumi is on her back in the bed. Her face is covered in sweat and she's pale. I grab the pillow from my bunk and tuck it under her leg so her foot is suspended in the air. I don't bother removing the first dressing, just fold one from the kit over top and tie it. It doesn't soak through right away, which surprises me. I pull a blanket over her. "I'm going to go get my dad."

Sumi shakes her head. "It's too dark. You'll get lost."

I think about how black the water looked that first night, no lights, nothing to mark the way. I say, "There's a moon tonight."

"There could be frigging stage lighting and you'd still get lost."

"You could tell me the way."

"And you'd still get lost."

"You can draw me a map."

"Shit, Lucas," she snaps. "It's not like there are signs—turn left at Pine Forest, second left at Salmon Creek. This coastline is like a broken comb. Everything looks the same. Sometimes even I get turned around. You could use up all your fuel wandering around like a fart in a glove."

I've heard my father use that expression. I say, "You need a doctor, Sumi."

She puts her hands over her face and moans, "Obviously."

"I could try. If I can't find Dad, I'll come back."

"No. Your old man should be here first thing in the morning. If not, we'll figure out something else. But you're not going anywhere until it gets light."

I sit down on the floor beside her bunk. "Sumi, I'm sorry."

"You're an idiot."

"I am. You're absolutely right."

"I know I'm right. And you sound like an idiot too."

I open my mouth to say something but decide to shut up.

She says, "You are the biggest idiot on the planet."

I nod.

"You do not belong here."

"I don't."

"You don't have the first clue about what it's like to live here. You don't respect what it takes."

It sounds like she's crying, and I know better than to look. Finally she says, "I never should have fired it."

I take a chance and turn to her. I make a move to brush a tear from her cheek but she holds her hand up to stop me.

She says, "And I actually pointed it at my foot."

Since I have nothing to lose, I say, "Well, you missed a good chunk of it."

She glares at me and then says, "Good thing I'm a terrible shot."

Now she lets me wipe away her tears. She says, "You're wasting lamp oil."

I snuff the lantern. Sumi is quiet. I know she's not sleeping because of the way she's breathing. After a long time I say, "You want some water or something?"

But she doesn't answer.

## Chapter Ten

I wish it were my foot. Then the pain would be concrete. Busted bone and scraps of flesh, that's real. This pain I feel is just a never-ending feeling of guilt. I must have fallen asleep though, because now the cabin is light. Sumi is lying with her eyes open, looking at the window.

"Fog," she says.

I get up and last night's Kahlúa ricochets inside my skull. I blink, then walk over to the window. It's all white and I rub the glass. Still nothing. I open the front door and step out onto the porch. The air feels like I'm inside a cloud. I can barely see the steps.

My stomach does a slow roll. No way will Dad be out in this. He'll take one look at the fog and go back to bed. Now anger boils in my gut. If he had stayed like he was supposed to, none of this would have happened.

I almost fall down the steps and turn to where the outhouse should be, except the whole world has disappeared. I walk a few paces down the path and turn back to the cabin. I can barely see it. In the fog, even sound is different. It's like everything is inside my head. I take a leak right where I'm standing and I know Sumi is right, I don't have what it takes for this place. I feel my way back to the cabin.

Sumi is just the way I left her. Her skin is pale and her hair seems to stick to her forehead. I start a fire in the stove and fill the kettle.

"Can I have a look at your foot?"

She doesn't respond, so I peel back the blanket. There's no more blood than last night, which is good. I put the blanket back. I find her staring at me and it makes me jump.

She says, "The fog won't lift for hours. Choppers won't fly, not in this."

"Yeah, but..."

"Shut up. You have to listen to me." Her voice is dead calm, and that scares me worse than her stare.

"Okay." I pull a chair over to the bed and sit down.

"You're going to take me to the logging camp. It's a bit farther but they have a medic and maybe even a helicopter already on the pad. We could go to my place but who knows when the chopper could get in."

I nod, not wanting to interrupt.

"I'm going to tell you how to find the camp. But you have to do this, Lucas. If you screw up and get us lost, I'm bear bait and you're next. No one is coming to find us."

I swallow. "Okay."

"Eat something if you want. Then take two fuel cans down to the dinghy."

I'm about to say that I can't even see the water, but she's still talking.

"Fog is like a wet blanket. Get yourself properly dressed this time. Put something on your head. I've got stuff you can use. Just find it."

It's like the effort of speaking wears her out. She sinks back onto her pillow.

Outside, it's like being blind, except that instead of black, everything is white.

I can barely see my feet, but I can tell from the gravel that I'm on the path down to the water. The fuel cans are outside the boat shed, and I load two into the wheelbarrow and then wheel down to the water. It takes a while to find the dinghy, but luckily I don't have to haul it too far to get it into the water. I load the fuel cans, then tie the dinghy well up on the shore. The rocks are wet, so I guess the tide is going out, but I'm not sure of anything.

When I get back to the cabin, I'm already tired. I dump everything out of my backpack onto my bunk and then go to Sumi's supplies and pack it with food and water. I grab my sleeping bag and warm clothes for both of us. Sumi doesn't say a word, just lies there looking straight up. I say, "Let's go," and I help her sit up. She leans on me to stand. She smells sour and her breath stinks. I'm sure I smell just as bad. I half carry her to the porch and then help her into the wheelbarrow. I jam the backpack and sleeping bag in around her.

"What do we need all this crap for?" she says. She's about to toss out the sleeping bag but I reach over and pull it back on top of her. She grumbles but leaves it alone.

When we get to the water, I can't get the wheelbarrow onto the rocks, so I have to practically carry Sumi to the dinghy. I untie it and take the oars. Only thing is, I can't see the fishing boat. I know where it must be, but the fog is so thick it's like there's nothing out there.

Sumi grunts, "I'll point. You row."

"You can see the boat?"

She shakes her head. "No. But I know where it is."

I'm beginning to wonder how the hell I'm going to find the logging camp. Maybe her foot isn't so bad. Maybe we should just wait it out. The fog will lift, and Dad will show up, and he can drive us to get help. But Sumi is the color of fog. We can't wait. She motions with her hands which way I should steer and, sure enough, I crash into the fishing boat, again. I hold the dinghy against the fishing boat so that Sumi can haul herself into the bigger boat. I try to ignore the words she calls me as I help push her butt into the boat.

I tie the dinghy to the mooring buoy, then clamber into the fishing boat. Sumi has taken a spot on the bottom facing back. She's using the backpack to hold up her injured foot. I toss her the sleeping bag and she wraps it around her shoulders. I pull up the hood on my floater coat and cinch it down around my face. Sumi tells me how to start the engine and I manage to get it going, then put it in gear.

Sumi closes her eyes and then motions with her hand, indicating which way I should steer. "Yesterday we fished toward open water. Today we're going the other direction and then up an inlet."

I nod. How hard could this be?

"Keep the shoreline on your left so it is just barely visible. At full throttle, it will take us just over two hours."

I mentally calculate lunch at the logging camp—a big plate of pancakes or whatever lumberjacks eat. They'll have a satellite phone, and I'll call my father and tell him he's a prick, although he probably already knows this.

"But with this visibility, we can't go more than quarter speed," she says.

I do the math. "That's like eight hours!"

"The inlet is peppered with deadheads, logs from the camp that get waterlogged and sink just out of sight under the water. Nail a deadhead and you'll be lucky if you're rowing home."

I set the throttle to the speed Sumi says. This speed feels dead slow. The only good thing is that there's less spray.

"You have to listen," she says, "and I mean really listen, for the sound of water breaking. If you hear that, you're coming up on the shore, and that's a bad thing."

Yes, driving a boat onto the rocks is a bad thing. So, watch for invisible deadheads and listen for an invisible shoreline.

"There are some shallow spots. I'll try to let you know when we're getting close."

Oh good.

"And don't waste fuel. You steer like you're drunk. Keep us heading straight."

I sigh. "Anything else?"

"It won't be for a while yet, but when you see the old Haida village on your right, you have to veer left. The inlet splits there and you'll be up your ass if you go the wrong way."

See an old village? Like I can see anything on shore right now. I say, "You're making this sound so easy."

She shifts her injured foot, grimacing with pain. "For most people, it would be."

# Chapter Eleven

I don't know if the fog is lifting or if I'm just getting used to it. I manage to steer around two deadheads. It's like the log is standing on its end in the water and just the tip sticks out, so you don't see it until you're practically on top of it. Each hour we're out we see more deadheads, and that's good, because it means we're getting closer to the camp.

My legs are sore from pulling in the halibut yesterday. So I sit, and then my butt is sore from sitting. And my hand is sore from steering the outboard. Cold is starting to creep in around the neck of my jacket. My feet are warm enough, thank goodness, because I'm wearing two pairs of heavy wool socks inside my rubber boots.

Which makes me think, why isn't Sumi's foot cold? She was wearing only one pair of socks when she shot herself. I look over at her. Her face is a weird color, somewhere between green and gray. I say, "You warm enough?"

She doesn't respond right away, and when she does, it takes her a while to focus on my face. "I'm fine."

Shit. She is not fine. I try to remember what happens to people when they've been injured. Shock, that's it, and it can kill you. You're supposed to keep the person warm and reassure them.

Oh, yeah, and call 9-1-1. I say, "Maybe get right into the sleeping bag. I'll help you." I make a move toward her but she growls.

She sits without speaking, then says, "When I was born, my hair was jet-black, my mother said, like my grandmother's. Then it grew in brown."

I wait for her to say something more, but she leans her head back and closes her eyes.

"You have beautiful hair," I say.

I don't think she's listening to me. When she finally speaks, her voice is soft and I have to lean forward to hear her. "She said she was going to be fine, that it was just a bad virus, and that I shouldn't come to the hospital. They loaded my mother onto the gurney and she joked that she'd be home before I got out of bed. But she died. She had diabetes and it messed up her heart. She didn't know."

"How old were you?"

"Fourteen. My grandmother's birthday card was on the table. Fourteen bucks, one for each year." Her voice sounds almost slurred. She says, "The cops came the next day. They thought someone had told me she died."

I was fourteen when my parents split. But I still had my parents. "I cannot imagine how hard that was."

"My grandmother is diabetic too. At least she knows." Her head lolls around like she's falling asleep.

"Sumi?" I want her to keep talking. I lean forward and give her a nudge.

She seems startled. "My mother never came back here. It was your dad who made it home for me."

Mom and I were gone. Dad was here. Maybe this always has been home for him.

Sumi gets quiet again, like she's fallen asleep. I look around. In the gloom of the fog, it seems to be getting dark. I can just make out a clearing on the shoreline. There are no buildings, not that I can see, but there are old totem poles leaning over, which tells me this must be the old Haida village. I wait until the boat is even with the village and then veer left.

# Chapter Twelve

It is definitely getting dark. It's colder too. We've been out here for hours and Sumi hasn't eaten anything. I think she's sleeping, or I hope so. I tip the last of a box of raisins into my mouth and cram the package in my pocket. Normally raisins disgust me. I've slowed the engine because Sumi said something about shallows and we should be heading into low water again. I think. Not that I know where the shallows are. I just hope I'm going in the right direction.

My dad told me once he likes to fish the shallows. I don't remember him talking to me about anything except fishing. He talks to me like I've been fishing with him, like I should know what he's talking about. Maybe he gets me mixed up with Sumi.

There's probably a way to tell when the outboard needs gas, but I'm not taking a chance on running it dry. I turn off the engine and reach for one of the gas cans.

Without the engine it is weirdly quiet. Sumi stirs and looks around. "Are we there?"

I tell her no, and she sets her head back without saying another word. I manage to fill the tank without spilling too much—and nowhere it will combust, I hope—when I hear a sound off the side of the boat.

I peer into the gloom. It's not water on rocks, so we're not heading aground. Then I hear a *pip*, almost like a chirp. The water beside the boat ripples. Then the water mounds, black and shiny. And I see a fin.

At first I think it's a whale because it's black and white, but it's too small to be a whale. It must be a porpoise, and there are a few of them. They rise in twos and threes, first on one side of the boat, then the other. They seem perfectly synchronized, moving through the water like dolphins at the aquarium. I hear a racket of splashing ahead of them and think about Sumi's story of the fish jumping.

I'm about to start the outboard again when it dawns on me. What are porpoises doing this far up the inlet? They'd be out in open water, wouldn't they?

When I changed direction at the village, did I take us back out toward sea? I'm starting to hyperventilate.

Ebb tide, so the water should be flowing out of the inlet. Is it ebb? This morning the beach was wet, like the water was receding. Since then, it would have flowed back in and now be heading out again. But maybe we've been out longer than I think. Except then it would be darker.

Maybe the porpoises are up the inlet to fish. They could be following the salmon heading back into the rivers. And maybe, like the old man, they're fishing the shallows.

If we're in the shallows, it's a good thing I didn't blast through. I start the engine but keep the RPMs low. I have no idea how much water we're in. I pass the porpoises, but they stay where they are. I take that as a good sign and give the engine a bit more gas. I glance over at Sumi and find her staring at me. Her gaze is so intent I'm not sure she's really looking at me. Then she says, "Your dad wouldn't have kept that hali either."

# Chapter Thirteen

I'm happy she's awake because I really need her help. "Sumi, you've got to have a look around, tell me where we are. I think we passed the shallows but I'm not sure."

"You're strong, like Denny. You have a strong heart."

The way she's talking reminds me of drunken girls at parties. Not that I'm immune to drunken girls at parties. Right now, though, I'd like to know we're not going to pile up on the shore. "That's fascinating, Sumi. Could you tell me where the hell we are?"

She blinks, peering out under her hood at the shoreline. She looks for a long time. "Keep the rocks to your right."

Instantly, as if she made it happen, two giant thumbs of rock appear ahead of us. There's plenty of room to go through them, but without even looking, she shakes her head at me. I steer around the rocks.

The rocks are like pillars. As we motor past them, on the other side, there must be fifty seals resting on a shoal between the rocks. There are seals in the water, their heads like black vinyl balls bobbing on the waves.

Her voice sounds like she has gravel in her throat. She says, "You better open it up."

"I can hardly see as it is, and it's getting dark."

She just looks at me.

"Don't call me an idiot," I say. But she's right. Once I lose the shoreline as a point of reference, I won't know how to steer.

She tells me to turn on the boat's running lights, and these give the faintest glow to the inside of the boat. She twists around in her seat, groaning. Her foot is bleeding again—in the gloom I can see a black puddle where she was resting it. She grabs the edges of the seat. I can see her shoulders moving up and down like she's breathing hard.

She turns her head toward me and says, "I'll point. You drive. Do exactly what I tell you."

It is like driving the boat inside a black sock. I don't bother looking at the water because if we're going to run into something, I'd rather not know.

I fix my stare on Sumi and watch where she points. Sometimes I hear her cursing, and I know I haven't exactly interpreted her bearing. We're bouncing off the waves, and spray nails us in the face. I squeeze my eyes almost closed. Driving fast, the air is so much colder and my fingers are frozen on the steering tiller. She motions wildly to steer left and I cut sharply, barely scraping past a log. How she saw it, I do not know. She's busy "steering" us back on course. Each time we hit a wave, her foot bounces. She's stopped cursing, which probably isn't good.

Now she's motioning me to slow down. Then we veer right, which freaks me out because it feels like we'll run straight into the shore. But then she points left into a cove, and suddenly the shoreline is punched with lights.

As we get closer, I see the logging camp and people walking around.

The docks are lit too, and I slow the boat a bit too late and bump Sumi one more time getting the boat alongside the dock. She's gone completely silent and her head hangs onto her chest.

A big guy in overalls takes my line and ties the boat up. He's looking at Sumi and I know he sees the blood. He pulls a radio from his pocket and instantly there are guys all over Sumi, carrying her down the dock, and more guys are running down to the docks.

I don't know what to do so I follow behind. My legs are stiff and I'm so cold my teeth are chattering. Somewhere, I hear a helicopter starting up.

The guys set Sumi on a board and strap her down. More guys appear, big guys, and they're carrying Sumi on the board, almost running with her.

I can't keep up, and the guy from the dock puts his hand on my shoulder. He seems to be talking to me but all

I can hear is the helicopter pounding in my head.

I try to run after Sumi, but now he grabs my jacket. He puts his face right up to mine and shouts at me to calm down.

I want to hit him, to push him away, but then I see the chopper, its bright lights appearing over the roofs of the buildings, then getting higher, and the noise dropping as it gets farther away.

# Chapter Fourteen

Last night, after the helicopter left, someone showed me to an empty bunk and gave me a blanket. I thought I wouldn't sleep but I must have. This morning I followed a well-worn path to the cook trailer. It's bright with morning sun and the tables are empty, so it looks like I've slept through breakfast.

At the table nearest the kitchen the big guy from the dock is hunched over an enormous bowl. I sit down across from him. His face is one inch from the bowl and he's shoveling in the food. It looks like eggs and hash browns with bits of bacon, and everything is laced with hot sauce. My stomach rumbles.

The cook comes out with another bowl, sees me and slides it across the table to me. I start to protest about taking his breakfast, but he holds his hand up as if to say, Just eat.

So I eat. The cook's name is Dylan, from the name tag on his uniform, and he makes a fine breakfast bowl. "Cilantro," I say. "Nice touch."

He looks at me, both eyebrows raised. "You cook?"

I finish my mouthful. "I want to." The cilantro surprises me at a logging camp this side of nowhere. I pour myself a coffee from a carafe on the table and add a dollop of real cream. Somehow I'm beginning to feel human.

Another guy comes into the trailer. He slips off a small backpack and sits down with us. Dylan pours him a coffee and says, "How was Vancouver?"

Now I recognize him—he's the medic. I remember him from last night, working on Sumi. I slop coffee over the rim of my cup. "How is she?"

He looks at me. "Sumi is surprisingly good, actually."

I have to set down my coffee, my hands are shaking so badly. "What about her foot?"

"They were taking her into the operating room when I left her last night." He adds cream and a stream of sugar to his coffee. "What I want to know is how you managed to get her here."

I really don't have an answer. I say, "She seemed to know the way."

The guy from the dock grins, and something about him makes me wonder just how well he knows her.

I say, "I guess she comes here a lot."

"Don't worry," Dylan says, and he eyes the guy from the dock. "Sumi doesn't come to see Leo. She brings us her limit, trades us fresh salmon for provisions. Somehow she resists Leo's stunning looks and table manners."

The medic laughs and gets up. He offers me his hand. "You must have inherited your father's internal GPS. He can find his way along this coastline blindfolded."

"I think it was luck."

"Well then, it was lucky for Sumi." He shakes my hand. "She's at Vancouver General Hospital, probably will be for a while." Then he leaves.

Leo offers to take a boat with me back to the lodge so I don't get lost, but I want to go on my own. The sea is flat calm and there's no fog, so it should be an easy trip. And it is. In the bright clear light of morning, the inlet looks completely different from yesterday, but strangely the same. It's like the landscape has soaked into me. At the rock pillars I slow down. The seals bark at me from the shoal. No porpoises today. Past the shallows I open it up again, standing in the boat to steer.

When I get close to the lodge, I see the deer on the grass, feeding. It's weird, arriving back here alone. I'm trying not to think about Sumi, how she's doing— and what they're doing at the hospital.

I tidy up the fishing boat and then transfer into the dinghy. On the oars I feel stronger, although I'm sure Sumi would still have something to say about my steering. I pull the dinghy high up on the beach and tie it to a driftwood log. When I walk toward the lodge, the deer lift their heads and watch me, but they don't run off.

In Sumi's cabin I wash and dry the dishes. I wipe up dark blood from the floor. I straighten her bed. I bag the trash, including the last of the bread, so that nothing attracts mice, or the bear.

This makes me think of Sumi's deer. Her grandmother is going to need that deer. I retrieve the wheelbarrow from down at the beach and then head back to the generator hut. The deer is still there and doesn't look too beat up by the bear. I lower it into the wheelbarrow. Sumi's rifle is still on the ground. Carefully, I pick it up and put it in the wheelbarrow with the deer. Then I head back out to the front of the lodge. I see Dad's boat on the mooring. He's in the inflatable, motoring in to shore. I take a deep breath and head down to the water.

# Chapter Fifteen

He looks tired. He throws me the rope and I pull the boat in while he lifts the prop out of the water. I feel like a little kid again. I have to tell him what happened, but I just want it all to go away. He steps out of the boat and we each take a side and haul it up the beach. He ties it beside the other dinghy.

He goes over to the dinghy and checks my knot but he doesn't retie it.

My throat feels like it could stick closed. "Dad," I say, but nothing else will come out.

He says, "I heard."

Just then a helicopter flies in over the ridge, the same one we came in on.

He says, "The pilot let me know."

As the helicopter lands, we walk up to the lodge. I'm grateful for the noise of the chopper because I don't have to speak. But then the pilot shuts down the engine.

I just have to tell him. I have to tell him I screwed up, badly, and that it's all my fault.

The pilot is getting out, looking at me. He knows. Everyone knows. But then Dad says, "Sumi told the camp crew that it was a hunting accident."

I look at him and I know he doesn't believe it. I start to tell him but he interrupts me. He says, "Up here, hunting accidents happen all the time."

He's letting her have this half-truth, and me too. He says, "I should have been with you."

It's half an apology, but it will do. I say, "It's okay."

"No, I really wanted to be here. But Deirdre and her mother, they're all sick with that damn flu and I didn't feel I could leave."

I say, "It was good you stayed." I mean it too. "Sumi would want to know her family was being cared for."

He nods. "Apparently she was asking about you too."

I'm not sure what that means, but he grins so I guess it's good.

The pilot makes a point of checking his watch, and my father says to me, "You're on the next flight out of Sandspit."

"You're not going?"

"To Vancouver?" He shakes his head. "No, I'm going…"

"Home."

"Yes, home." He reaches into his jacket and hands me a printed boarding pass to Vancouver. "I've prepaid your ticket on to LAX. You just have to pick it up at the airport."

I wish he were a total stranger. It would be easier to feel this way, like the pain I'm so used to is just a feeling. Like he is nothing at all. But he's not. I say, "I've still got a few days. I could stay with you."

He rubs his hair and already I regret saying it. But then he says, "There's nothing I'd like better, Lucas, any other time."

He might mean it too.

On the flight into Vancouver, I show the guy sitting across the aisle the photo on my camera of the halibut. "You let it go?" he says, like I'm crazy.

When the plane lands, I follow the stream of people out to where family members are waiting, hugging and laughing, and I keep walking. At the SkyTrain, I pause just long enough to figure out where I'm going, and then I take a seat and wait for my stop: Vancouver General Hospital.

# Acknowledgments

With deepest appreciation to SH, KD and the writers of UBC CrWr509, and to Maureen in Haida Gwaii.

Diane Tullson has written numerous novels for teens, along with *Red Sea* and *The Darwin Expedition*. Diane lives in Delta, British Columbia.

# orca soundings

The following is an excerpt from
another exciting Orca Soundings novel,
*Masked* by Norah McClintock.

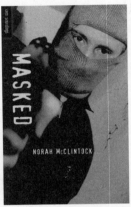

978-1-55469-364-1  $9.95 pb
978-1-55469-365-8  $16.95 lib

**WHEN DANIEL ENTERS A CONVENIENCE**
store on a secret mission, he doesn't expect
to run into anyone he knows. That would ruin
everything. When Rosie shows up, she's hoping
to make a quick getaway with her waiting
boyfriend. But the next person through the door
is wearing a mask and holding a gun. Now
things are getting complicated.

# Chapter One

"Uh, do you have a bathroom I can use?" I'm ready with an excuse for when the man behind the counter says no. I thought long and hard to come up with it. You have to when you're asking to use the bathroom in a convenience store, which doesn't have to provide one the way restaurants do. I have to get yes for an answer if my mission is going to be a success.

The man behind the counter scowls. He peers at me from under gray eyebrows that look like steel wool. Is he on to me? Does he suspect?

"What about your coffee and taquito?" he says. "Are you still going to want those?"

"Yeah. And a two-liter cola and the latest *Wrestling World*, if you have it." I throw those in to improve my chances of getting a yes.

"We have it. What about *Wresting Today*? You want that too?" His piggy little eyes drill into me. I see immediately where he's going. If I want to use the facilities, I'm going to have to cough up some more money. I take another glance at the magazine rack.

"And *Wrestling Connoisseur*," I say. What the heck—I'm getting paid enough. A few magazines aren't going to make a dent in my paycheck.

"Through the door beside the coolers and down one flight," the man behind the counter says.

As I head down the narrow aisle toward the coolers, I glance in the security mirror at the back of the store. The man at the counter, the owner, is watching me.

Going through the door beside the big Coke-sponsored cooler is like stepping from Oz back into Kansas. The tile floor in the store sparkles. The wooden floor on the other side of the door is dingy, scuffed and slightly warped. The lights in the store are blindingly bright. On the other side of the door there is only a single naked lightbulb that makes the places it doesn't hit look inky and a little spooky. The walls of the store are chock-a-block with neatly displayed and colorful products. The walls of the small room are bare except for a car dealership calendar that hangs from a nail directly above a battered old table and chair. On the table is an adding machine—I didn't even know those still existed. Next to it is a two-drawer olive green filing cabinet. On the wall, in an ancient fixture with a pull chain, is another naked light-bulb. This is where the owner does his accounts. To the left of the door is a flight of wooden stairs. But I don't go down it.

Instead, I listen. It's quiet in here. It's also quiet out in the store. I tiptoe over to the desk. I'd been expecting a computer, but there isn't one. I open the top drawer of the filing cabinet. It's jammed with files. I thumb through them, looking for the one I've been sent to find. I don't see it. I close that drawer, open the next one and thumb through more folders.

Bingo! There it is, neatly labeled.

I pull it out and scan the sheets inside. They look like the ones that were described to me. I dig the miniature camera—a spy camera, if you can believe it—out of my pocket and photograph every sheet. I put everything back into the folder and replace the folder in the file cabinet. I tuck the camera into my pocket. I start back to the door.

Before I get there, I hear the man behind the counter yell something—a name. I'm about to push the door open and go back into the store when I hear a different voice—a familiar one. This has never happened to me before. I decide to wait. If I go out there, I'll be recognized. If I'm recognized, I'll be exposed. If I'm exposed, I'll have to abort my mission. And if I abort…let's just say I don't want to kiss my paycheck goodbye.

# orca soundings

For more information on all the books
in the Orca Soundings series, please visit
**www.orcabook.com.**